A Good Kiss is Hard to Find

Augustine Lang

CHAPTER ONE

KITTY FAIRWELL HAD ALWAYS considered herself a romantic. What woman, after all, does not want to marry for love?

Still, she felt her friend Louisa's decision to elope with Harry Bastable was…ill-advised.

Or—not advised at all, really. Certainly, Louisa hadn't asked *Kitty's* advice.

But now Louisa had asked for Kitty's *help*, and Kitty was a Fearless Fairwell, wasn't she? Rescuing a friend from a blackguard of a fiancé might not be the same as the heroic military service that had earned her brothers their sobriquet, but Kitty wasn't about to let the men claim *all* the glory.

Louisa needed rescuing; she had called upon Kitty. Ergo, Kitty would rescue.

"*Where* are we going, exactly?" asked the least heroic of her brothers.

Will Fairwell was leaning against the inside of the carriage, looking wan. He got motion-sick. But, even as un-heroic as he was, he had agreed to fetch Kitty at the drop of a hat. Kitty's heart swelled with pride.

"To Grosvenor Chapel."

"Kitty, that's *just down the street*. You did not have me pack a bag so we could go to a *service*. And what's wrong with St. George's?"

"If you'd been quicker with the carriage, we wouldn't need to stop; but the Whalens and Miss Fettinger were returning from morning calls and I didn't want to have to explain Louisa to them. So I sent her around to the chapel with a footman. It seemed like a safe place for her to wait."

He gave her a long-suffering look. "You didn't want to explain *what* about Louisa to them? Is that your friend Miss Green?"

Kitty took a deep breath. If she couldn't get Will on her side, it was a lost cause.

"Miss Green was seduced by a blackguard, and he was violent toward her. So she threw him off and came to me for help."

His eyes widened. "She came to *you*?"

"I'm her closest friend in London." Kitty hesitated. "She's in Lady Hargrave's household. You think *she* would *not* have held Louisa at fault?"

He considered briefly, then grimaced.

"I think Lady Hargrave would tell *me* to push off if I so much as sneezed in her drawing-room. And she was always trying to get *me* married to one of her insufferable daughters."

Kitty caught sight of her maid, Jane, in the carriage seat beside her, rolling her eyes. She was confident it was in regards to Lady Hargrave rather than Will, so she let it go.

Will was awkward, and only the third son, but the Fairwells were *quite* rich enough that even the Lady Hargraves of the *ton* would overlook his want of a title, his reputation for being a pinch-penny, and his habit of running off at the mouth when nervous.

"I am so glad you catch my meaning," said Kitty tartly.

"Don't you think you ought to have trusted the Whalens?" Will tried dutifully. But even as he said it, his voice was full of doubt.

In the same way Louisa had been brought out by her relation Lady Hargrave, Kitty, also motherless, was living with her and Will's cousin Mrs Whalen whilst they were all in London for the season.

The Fairwell family ranged from harmlessly eccentric recluses (their father Patrick and brother Ned) to dashing rascal-cum-diplomat (Robert) to unimpeachable *bon ton* (their sister Susannah—and Kitty was taking a stab at it).

The Whalens, on the other hand, were *keenly* civilized—in the way of people who always have a niggling doubt about the security of their situation.

"The Whalens already don't like her. They think she's trying to marry for money. Which is *true*," Kitty added, since this was a sore spot with Will and she thought she'd better be honest from the start, "but so are *they*; they just have more to start with."

He groaned. But the carriage drew to a halt. They had reached the rather common chapel, a small red brick building with white pilasters at each corner and a portico held up by columns.

Will's stone-deaf valet Henry Astley glanced up from reading *Ackermann's*, raising a querying eyebrow. Will made a sign to him that he should stay.

"Get rid of the footman, if you please?" Kitty said.

Without waiting for confirmation, she slid out of the carriage and dashed up the steps. She trusted that Will would follow, and also that he wouldn't be a pinchpenny when it counted.

Just inside the door, she at once spotted the miserable-looking Miss Green attempting to hide behind an arrangement of daffodils on a pedestal. She was a tall young lady, wearing a peach-coloured cloak of the finest shimmering silk, with the hood up. Mrs Whalen's footman was standing as far apart from her as he could manage and still be reasonably defined as her escort. His frown declared, "This is *not* the business of a respectable footman."

Will—the best of all brothers!—sighed and went to go tip him.

Sniffling, Miss Green embraced Kitty gratefully.

"I told you I wouldn't desert you," Kitty whispered. "Come out —we have a carriage."

Will handed Louisa up into the carriage, but Kitty avoided him. Instead, she called a direction to the coachman.

"No, no, wait one second!" said Will on hearing. "Pardon me, we need to discuss this. *Kitty*."

He pulled Kitty to the open door and in a worried voice addressed Louisa through it. "Oughtn't we take you back to Lord and Lady Hargrave?"

Louisa leaned forward. "I've *been* back," she said in a low flat voice. She gestured to the small traveling valise at her feet. "I ran there from St. George's. Bastable followed me. He took great pleasure in telling Lady Hargrave exactly what had happened. And he said he would say it everywhere just to spite me. *He* had been willing to do the honourable thing. So it was my fault." She pushed her hood back and pointed at the hand-mark on her face, with deeper red marks as if from rings. "That was Lady Hargrave." She pushed one of her snug sleeves up with difficulty. "This was Bastable." Will flinched. "There are others, but I'd have to undress." Her voice was still completely devoid of feeling. "If you don't want to have anything to do with me I would understand, but please tell me where to go."

Will sighed. He stepped back and shouted to the coachman.

"As my sister said. Gatewood House."

Louisa Green was, Kitty thought with pity, really inconveniently beautiful. Luckily, Will was too carriage-sick to become besotted, or else he found himself unable to fancy a woman substantially taller than himself. That was good. Kitty had seen men become besotted with Louisa in under a minute, even when she kept her eyes firmly fixed on their boots—a not uncommon situation.

Kitty was in no way envious. She was satisfied with her own appearance when she looked in the mirror—she had bright eyes and a winsome nose. Usually when gentlemen complimented her, it was "what a charming smile you have, Miss Fairwell." She knew she was pretty and that was quite enough for her.

But Louisa was something else entirely. The only way anyone ever described Louisa was "beautiful."

It didn't matter that she was already twenty-one, and too tall, and flat-bosomed; she was always "that beautiful girl." She had a perfect fair complexion, widely-spaced grey eyes, and the face of a haunted angel. It was hard to talk to her without falling silent and simply admiring her beauty.

When Kitty had first met her, very soon after her debut, it had taken a few minutes even for *her* to recover from it. But she had pushed onward, because she felt sorry for the exquisitely beautiful, obviously shy young lady trying to hide behind a pillar at a ball. Miss Green had answered Kitty's friendly inquiries in a very soft voice.

In the ten minutes in which Kitty had first made her acquaintance, no fewer than three gentlemen had approached Miss Green. Miss Green stared at them with wide eyes and was unable to say anything. She looked at Kitty desperately.

Luckily, Kitty was quite good at managing things. She made free use of her fan to shoo them away, with a charming smile in case one of them wanted to dance with *her* later.

"Miss Green does not care to dance at the moment. She and I are conversing. Thank you *very* much."

Miss Green whispered to her, "*Thank you.* It's not that I don't like any of them. But it's so *loud.* I can't think."

"And they look at you as if they're wolves wanting to eat you, Little Red Riding Hood," said Kitty, because Mrs Whalen wasn't around to hear and be shocked.

Kitty had slipped away from Mrs Whalen as she fussed over an even richer woman who bored Kitty to tears. Kitty was making her way back—but she would do it in her own time.

Miss Green looked at her gratefully. "*Yes.*"

"Where's your chaperon? She ought to be fending off the unsuitable ones."

"Lady Hargrave suggested a few likely candidates." Louisa looked near tears. "But one of them made an inappropriate remark as we went to dance, and I…slipped away."

"Good for you," said Kitty stoutly. "Lady Hargrave, you say? I believe I saw her speaking with my cousin Mrs Whalen. Let's go remonstrate with the shameful job they're doing."

Kitty could never have imagined, at the time, how true those words would turn out to be! Horrendous Lady Hargrave!

Now, neither Will nor Louisa were inclined to talk. So Kitty gazed out the window during the long and largely silent carriage journey, lost in thought. How fortunate it was that she had declined to go calling this morning on account of finishing up a new novel.

True, she had missed out on seeing Percy Wolcott...oh dear, she was going to have to write to Percy...but had it not been so, how different things might have been for Louisa.

Gatewood had seemed to Kitty to be an obvious choice. Neither Bastable nor Lord and Lady Hargrave would be able to approach Louisa here. And unlike Grandbourne where Kitty had grown up, her brother Ned's estate Gatewood House was not so far from London as to be an excessively trying journey.

It was not a *jaunt*, to be sure, but something she could make sound reasonable to Will in the circumstances.

And, even more usefully—there were no ladies in residence to make trouble.

Kitty had not yet seen the villa except in sketches. She remembered her father and Will discussing its purchase about two years previous. Yet at the time, she had been in the handle of an unhealthy passion for Gothic novels, and judging a potential purchase on the quality of its crop yields—rather than on whether its grounds bore a grotto—seemed dreadfully boring.

Then, shortly thereafter, Ned had come home wounded, and went to ground there as a recluse. Which *was* rather Gothic, but certainly not the sort of thing she would have wished for any of *her* brothers.

She had seen Ned in London since, briefly, but the vaguely-promised visit to Gatewood had never transpired. And then she'd had her presentation at Court and become occupied with other things.

She would have hoped to see Gatewood at last under circumstances *not* involving a tragedy, but regardless, now that the carriage was taking the turning from the closest post town, Glenchester, she was pleased and a little excited.

When Will mumbled they were passing through the village, she peered eagerly out the window of the carriage. She was inclined by a generous nature to think well of the place. But how charming it truly was! How quaint! They rattled past a stone church and a few houses. Then they slowed, as if the driver were looking for a landmark.

"Are we near?" Kitty asked.

Will refused to look out the window. "The gate has two stone towers—I mean little ones—not something dramatic, don't get excited—with ivy all over. That's the turn to the drive. I don't think he can miss it."

And indeed almost as soon as he'd spoken, the carriage turned. Kitty caught a glimpse of a short squat gate tower flash by, tawny-coloured stone under masses of ivy. Then a patch of woodland, cut through by the drive up which they rattled. Kitty leaned her head out the window as far as she could. Will, being the fine brother he was, did not reproof her. Or perhaps he did, and she simply didn't hear him.

There it was!

Having outgrown her Gothic moment—she now considered it a trifle childish—Kitty was not at all disappointed by her first sight of Gatewood House.

True, as country manors went, it was modest in size. A villa, really; not intended as someone's main residence. But it had a wonderfully pleasing, *charming* effect, which (at the mature age of nineteen) she now more appreciated. The villa was pale gold stone, with tall windows on the ground floor and small square windows on the shorter upper story. Above the central door was a portico supported by four simple columns in the style of a Greek temple.

From their slantwise angle of approach, Kitty could see that what would have looked like a flat front if viewed dead-on was actually a central squarish building with an added narrow wing extending off the side. Since the house was symmetrical, she imagined that the other side had been extended in the same way.

"Is it very old? It looks like something from Greece."

"The main part of the house is about ninety years old—the wings were finished just a few years ago. Actually—" Will sounded wry "—they *weren't* finished, on the inside. I wasn't privy to the details, but I suspect the cost of wings might rather be part of the reason the Eckerleys, er, found it a good idea to sell. I gather the younger Edward Eckerley intended a library in one wing and a portrait gallery in the other, but spent more than he should have on the *books* and the *portraits*, and by the time the wings were done, he'd dug himself in too deep. I was happy to buy—I mean, father and I were—"

Kitty was as always amused by Will's staunch adherence to the polite fiction that father cared a fig about managing the business end of the Fairwells' estate.

"It's good land here—and the Eckerleys were *delighted* to have ready money. So I believe we—"

Kitty could hear the driver calling "Whoaa," to the horses. The carriage rattled to a stop at the same time Will did:

"—we all thought we came out ahead."

He looked at the floor and sighed. "Well—here we are, then. Give me a moment, if you will."

Quick as a wink he had hopped out of the carriage. Kitty could hear him speaking to the driver, though she couldn't make out what he was saying. As she was straining to hear, she instead caught Louisa's soft, exhausted-sounding words.

"Kitty, thank you so much. You and your brother are so kind. I truly don't know what I would have done without you."

"*Will* is kind," said Kitty, "but Ned is likely to sulk. You mustn't mind him; he growls like a wolf but is really more of a grumpy collie."

Five minutes later Kitty was glad she'd given that warning. They stood in the unfurnished entry hall of Gatewood House, a large echoing cube with deep red walls and a glossy floor of grey and white diamond tiles. She knew it echoed, because the sharp little hisses of Ned and Will arguing on the far side, in vehement undertone, were underscored by an extra reverberation of sound against the empty walls.

At other times Kitty would have liked to wade in and argue herself, but Louisa was looking an inch from tears and Kitty didn't wish to abandon her. Louisa had pulled up the hood of her cloak again. All Kitty could see was the edge of her profile, her mouth set hard.

Kitty put her arm around her friend's waist. Louisa's body was full of tension as if she were ready to bolt.

"Only a grumpy collie, I *promise*," Kitty murmured.

Louisa's mouth trembled upward into the faintest of smiles.

Despite Ned's grumpiness, Kitty was so happy to see him. It had been—goodness, had it been almost four months? And he looked so much better than he had! He was still walking with a cane, of course—it had been a miracle his leg had been saved at all—but he moved with some of the nervous energy of old, rather than the tense repressed care of someone fighting through pain. Really she was quite *heartened* by the way he was wiggling the top of his cane in punctuation to whatever he was growling at Will. He shot a frown in the direction of the two girls; Kitty smiled at him; he seemed not to know how to respond, so he quickly looked back at Will.

"What happened to your brother's eye?" Louisa whispered. "May I ask?"

"Boney, of course," Kitty said, with understandable pride, "on the peninsula."

"Does it pain him?" Louisa whispered. "Poor man."

"He told me the eye has never hurt at all, thank goodness." Kitty didn't add that whatever fragment of shot had deadened Ned's now filmy-white eye had not likewise deadened the feeling of the angry red scars extending up to his temple.

Ned limped toward them abruptly, a foul expression on his face; Kitty could feel Louisa tense again. Behind Ned, Will threw up his hands. Then he moved forward, easily passing Ned. Will came to a stop at Kitty's side, as if prepared to defend her.

The two brothers could hardly have looked less alike. They

were, officially, half-brothers. Despite the slightly-skewed stoop Ned had acquired, he was still nearly a full foot taller and at least three stone heavier than small, spry Will. Kitty and Will both had their mother's curly brown hair with glints of gold, but Ned had straight black hair, thinning at the top. Will's face was all points, fox-like, whilst Ned had somehow, despite everything, kept his round boyish cheeks. His heavy straight black brows were currently furled together. The left brow was shorter than the right, cut through by a scar. Kitty still had her arm around Louisa's back; she could feel her breathing hard. She gave her a little squeeze of encouragement.

"I'm so very glad to see you, Ned," Kitty said with absolute truth, "and you're looking well. I beg your pardon for arriving unannounced; you know I never would have had it not been an emergency. Thank you so much for putting up with us whilst I help Miss Green get things sorted out."

Ned opened his mouth. He glanced at Louisa. His mouth stayed open. He went from looking fierce to looking stupid in the course of a single second.

Whether it was because of what Kitty had said (she doubted it) or because Ned was, deep down, too much a gentleman to complain in the face of a girl needing help, he just shut his mouth with a clack of teeth.

"Welcome, Miss Green," he said, sounding as if he deeply grudged it. He looked around behind him. "Oh, *there* you are, John," he said with relief.

Kitty glanced to follow his gaze. A slim man of twenty-five or so had come quietly to one of the doors. He was raising his eyebrows at the scene before him, though between his tarnished-blond hair and tan skin, his eyebrows were hardly visible, so the expression was more of a charming moue.

Will said, "Ah, good day, Mr Stanger." He too sounded relieved.

"Good day, Mr Fairwell," said Mr Stanger, with a polite inclination of his head. "It's a pleasure to see you again." But his eyebrows were still up. Coming forward, he looked at Ned, at Kitty for a moment, and then at Louisa, taking his time absorbing everything as Will started to natter a quick introduction.

Kitty gave Louisa another squeeze and released her. She extended her hand.

"Oh, but I do know you, Mr Stanger—or *of* you. Thank you for being such a good friend to my brother."

Her brother's friend was—well, he was interesting to look at. His face was long and lean with a narrow chin, but any harshness was kept at bay by a generous, almost feminine mouth that seemed well-suited to smiling. He was smiling at her now, and bending his head slightly so as not to tower over her and Will. He wasn't as tall as Ned; it was merely that most people were taller than they. He was built slim but his shoulders looked strong under his dark blue coat.

She smiled back at him. Then she realized, startled, that he wore his hair long, and tied back at the nape of the neck.

"Ah, well—" said Mr Stanger, "it's merely what friends do—take care of each other."

Beside him, Ned flapped a hand up and rolled his eyes as if in exasperation. Mr Stanger had vanquished his argument about Louisa's presence without even being aware of it. Mr Stanger glanced at him, still with the eyebrow-less raised brow. Kitty pressed her lips together, trying not to show her amusement.

Ned said sharply: "John, will you be so good as to see that my family and Miss Green have somewhere to rest. God knows where."

"You *did* get that furniture I sent..." said Will. Out of the corner of her eye, Kitty saw him turning around on his heel to look around the room. None of it was apparent.

"We did, and thank you for it," Mr Stanger hastened to say. He had a firm quiet way about him, with observant eyes as if searching for ways to ease other people's discomforts. "There are some usable bedrooms upstairs. I'll have the housekeeper get a few ready. In the meantime—perhaps the saloon?"

"*I* will be in the library," said Ned. And with a scrape of his foot and a clack of his cane he had turned and headed off across the hall.

Kitty almost called after him, disappointed to lose his company even if he was being a malcontent. But, on the other hand, Louisa had relaxed as soon as he'd turned away.

"Through here?" asked Kitty stoutly, gesturing to the open doorway directly across from the entry door. It was an easy guess, being flanked by columns and roofed by a pediment. Everything important these days seemed to have columns!

CHAPTER TWO

THE VILLA WAS BUILT AROUND a staircase hall in the centre. As they passed through, Kitty saw that the doors to the left and right were closed, so she could not discern where they led. Without pausing, they went straight through to the saloon at the back of the house.

The saloon was dreadfully cold. It was furnished in a manner that Kitty thought of as "haphazard" even at the slightest glance; blue upholstery on one couch, red on another, and surely no one had ever matched *those* chairs with *that* table! And it was sorely wanting for pleasant adornment. There was not a single statue, nor vase, nor painting.

A single brave parlour palm leaned toward the curtains covering the far wall; its steadfastness gave Kitty hope. Perhaps when the curtains were opened there would be a prospect.

Mr Stanger had gone to speak to the servants. Someone must have made an educated guess, however, as a young maid was already lighting the fire with a tinderbox.

"What sort of furniture *did* you send, Will?" Kitty teased. "If there were ever a house in need of a woman…!"

"It's better than it was *last* time I was here," he said feebly.

When the fire caught, and the maid took her leave with a curtsey—looking at both Kitty and Louisa with wide eyes—Kitty settled Louisa in a chair near to the fire-screen. She huddled toward it gratefully.

Now that she was at rest, Kitty could see that her self-control was slipping. Kitty knelt beside her and they made a whispered consultation. Kitty rose, and murmured to Will in turn. She didn't know John Stanger well enough to assume whether he was the sort of man who would see "guests" and think "tea."

As it transpired, he was. When Will returned with the maid,

bearing not only tea but a supper of cold meats, he was able to reassure Kitty that a tray could also be found in what was to be Louisa's room.

Supper, or was it indeed a meagre dinner? Kitty didn't know what hours the household kept, and she didn't have a high hope of Ned entertaining in style.

She cast a longing, thirsty glance at the steaming teapot. But she resisted.

"You be mother. I'll be right back."

She settled Louisa in her room, coaxing her out of her dress and into a bed shift and night-cap. She bit her lip now having a full view of Louisa's bruises. Louisa began to cry silently.

"Into bed with you," Kitty said with forced cheer. She wasn't unused to dealing with other people's doldrums; on the contrary; but it wasn't something she had ever become comfortable with. If that were possible. A sad familiar feeling stirred in her stomach.

To cover up, she cosseted Louisa as much as she could, pouring her tea the way she liked it, bringing her a cloth to wipe her face, insisting that she eat a few bites. She stroked her hair. "It's over now; you're safe, my dear."

By the time Louisa was in bed with a blanket up to her nose, Kitty was parched and ravenous. She closed the door as quietly as she could and then positively dashed down the stairs and back to the saloon.

She wouldn't have minded being seen in such a state of dishevelment by her brothers, but when she came to a hard halt in the door of the saloon, she discovered that not only Ned and Will but Mr Stanger were arrayed around one of the oval tables eating. Mr Stanger looked over at her. She blushed. She hadn't remembered to so much as check her appearance in Louisa's mirror.

Mr Stanger started to rise.

"No, no, don't get up," Kitty said hastily.

She forced herself to keep her head held high and not even so much as glance at what had to be *her* teacup, now probably full of cold tea. She crossed to the room's single mirror and confirmed at once that her curls were hopeless. Should she fight a losing battle whilst a stranger looked on? No. She took a deep breath, and returned to the table with dignity. This time, she accepted the chair Mr Stanger leapt to pull out for her.

Will serenely reached for the teapot and filled her teacup with steaming tea. Kitty felt inexpressibly loved.

She drank her first cup with as much a balance between dignity and thirst would allow. Will at once refilled it without comment. Kitty beamed across the table at Mr Stanger. Tea made everything better.

"May I ask how your friend fares?" asked Mr Stanger quietly.

Kitty hesitated. She found herself trusting, in his gentle inquiry of concern, that he was not going to judge Louisa too harshly.

"Her spirits are low," she had to confess.

Ned snorted. "Little wonder. Please, tell us the history of Miss Green. Will, in a fit of chivalry, has left it to you, beyond muttering 'seduced by a rascal.'"

"I don't *know* the whole story," said Will. His eyes pled forgiveness from Kitty.

"Must we really discuss this whilst eating?" Kitty said, pleading a bit herself.

"The sooner the better," Ned said, "since I need to decide what to do with her. Why is she under my roof?"

"Ah, should I excuse myself?" said Mr Stanger hastily.

Ned addressed his response to Kitty rather than Mr Stanger. "He'll end up thinking better of her if he hears it from *you*—than if I tell him later."

Kitty sighed. "I never know if you're jesting or not."

"Never. I leave that to John."

"Oh, and that *was* a jest!" she said.

"*Talk*," growled Ned.

"Well it's—" Kitty didn't know where to begin. What details would they find necessary, and what would they rather not know?

"It's her first season; we met each other almost at the beginning. She hasn't a mother either, so she was brought out by Lady Hargrave, who is a relation on her father's side. Do you know Lady Hargrave?"

Ned grimaced. "Regrettably."

"She finally got all her daughters married," said Will *sotto voce*, "thank heavens."

"That's why Lady Hargrave waited so long to bring out Louisa," said Kitty tartly, "she wanted them to have half a chance."

"I don't care," said Ned. "Please get to the point."

"Stories just take as long as they take!" said Kitty. "But if you want the shortest form, Will told you already. She was seduced by Harry Bastable, and he beat her, and she asked me for help getting away from him, and I gave it. You would have done the same thing."

"Probably not. Is 'seduced' the euphemism for forced, or was she complicit?"

Kitty gritted her teeth. "She was under the impression he intended to marry her."

She did not add: Eventually. *Eventually*, Louisa had talked him into it. And they'd had to wait until she was twenty-one, in any case, because she didn't have any living parents to give consent.

"So she's just stupid," said Ned curtly.

"They were to be married this morning, *in fact*," Kitty said, feeling this was a cutting point.

"Let me guess; his family put a stop to it. By the by, did you know about all this as it was going on?"

"*No*," she snapped. "Well. She mentioned when he first paid her attention. But she didn't talk about him after that. Please don't insult me. And it *wasn't* his family."

"Does she have money?" Ned inquired blandly.

Kitty had to say "No." All of Louisa's fine clothing had been Lady Hargrave's doing.

"Then they objected."

"Perhaps they did; but as far as I know they didn't have anything to do with it."

"So if they were going to be married, why didn't it come off?"

"Because they argued and he hit her," said Kitty crossly, "and she wasn't going to marry him after that; and if you say a word to the contrary I'll throw tea in your face." She tested it. "And it's hot."

Hot enough that she would probably aim for his chest. But still, she *would*.

She stared him down. Ned snorted but didn't say anything.

"I saw her bruises, Ned," said Will softly, looking down at his tea. "She'd probably take her cloak off and show you too, but you *aren't* going to ask her. You hear me?"

Will seldom put his foot down, but on the vanishingly rare occasions he did, no one dared gainsay him. Or perhaps they were just too startled.

Or perhaps it was that he was the one who distributed the allowances.

"I have no desire to," said Ned. Then he pushed the matter as far as he could without getting tea in his face. "What did they argue about?"

"*I don't care*," said Kitty violently.

Will was still looking down at his teacup as if he was afraid to meet Ned's eyes. But he held up a single warning finger in his brother's direction. "And neither do you."

"Did you just stand up for yourself twice in two minutes?" Ned inquired. "I'm overwhelmed."

"Go to hell," said Will, firmly but without much heat, in the direction of the teacup.

Mr Stanger leaned forward and gave Ned a sharp warning look, which Kitty recognized as cousin to the one Susannah used to give Robert when his jesting went too far.

Ned abruptly helped himself to more cold chicken as if that had absolutely been what he'd planned to do all along.

Kitty found this quite interesting. Even when young, Ned had never made an effort to be charming. After his injuries, all the worst parts of his temper had come out. Remonstrating with him whilst he was in a pet usually made things worse, not better.

If Mr Stanger not only felt safe glaring at her brother, but it had an *effect*—Kitty was impressed!

She decided to take the opportunity to change the conversation. She turned toward Ned with a smile. Not *false* cheer, but certainly cheer carefully husbanded. "You know I'm sorry about the circumstances of our visit, Ned. But, despite them, I'm grateful to be here now. I haven't seen you since Christmas! I wish you would come visit us when we're in London. It's not *too* far."

"Carriages hurt," said Ned shortly.

She should have remembered.

"Oh. Yes, I'm sorry." She tried again, with a glance in the other direction. "Well, Will, you should bring me! I know you don't like travel either, but it doesn't seem to stop you! We could come during the Summer."

Will looked uncomfortable, though that was his usual state. "If Ned wants guests, that's up to him."

"I do *not*," growled Ned, "especially if you insist on bringing strays with you."

Kitty felt her composure stretch. She could have caught it—she saw it being pulled—but she let it snap. Then it was done, and out of her control.

"Strays!" she said sharply. "Do not speak of my friend like that. If someone had used me ill, you would hope any stranger would give me aid; and you can hardly expect better from a stranger than you are willing to do yourself."

"I expect nothing whatsoever from strangers," said Ned flatly.

"That is a sad thing. But I still, I will *always* take exception to my friend being subject to a term of abuse from my brother's lips. She is not a stray, like a dog or a cat; she is a feeling woman."

"She's right, Ned," said Will quietly; "it was ill said."

Ned made as if to get to his feet, but he fumbled his cane. It clacked against the leg of his chair. He looked down, but Kitty could see the utter frustration in his face.

In a calm, quiet, but inexorable voice, Mr Stanger said: "Ned, simply a word of apology will do."

Ned sat down again slowly.

"Very well. I apologize. She is a feeling woman, but she undeniably has strayed." His black eyes fixed on Kitty. "She has people. Summon them with all speed before her deeds affect your chances. Because I know catching a husband is important to you."

There was a day when she would have quailed from any argument, but somehow in the last year she had become an adult. Perhaps it had been the day she'd become engaged.

She met Ned's gaze.

"I would marry *no* man who would demand that I place a friend's reputation above her safety."

"You would find that most husbands would demand their wives show better discernment in their choice of friends. As, indeed, I as your older brother must demand of you. She must write to Lord and Lady Hargrave. They must understand that she is their responsibility. And you will get me their direction, or I will get it from her myself."

"*Not* Lady Hargrave," said Kitty. Oh dear, she hadn't explained that part. "The Hargraves have—thrown her off." Ned gave her a vile look; she had to make a peace offering. "But perhaps—Miss Horne. Louisa's aunt. She raised her since her parents died. *She* will stand by her."

Kitty was not indeed *entirely* certain if this were the case.

She couldn't deny that Miss Horne had been a most determined advocate for Louisa.

When Mr Green had married against his family's wishes, he'd been cut off from his inheritance. He'd had to work, and he and his wife and Louisa had struggled to get by. There was no chance that Louisa would inherit what should have been Mr Green's portion, but Miss Horne had worked most fiercely on his sister Lady

Hargrave's sympathies (or guilts) to see that Louisa could at least be brought out. "Let not the sins of the father—and so on," Kitty had heard her say.

Louisa had never expressly *said* that Miss Horne was counting on Louisa's uncanny beauty to make a rich match. Nevertheless, from Miss Horne's constraints upon Louisa, and the coolness between niece and aunt, Kitty had slowly come to understand it to be the case.

The knowledge had discomfited her. But it *was* what women did, and until Louisa had asked for help, Kitty had with some reluctance considered it none of her business. She had merely hoped that Louisa would find a propertied man whose character was good and whom she liked. And that had seemed entirely possible, given the wide range of gentlemen who had pursued her.

"So write to Miss Horne," said Ned impatiently. "Again, I don't care who takes her, as long as she goes away. The mail coach passes through Glenchester at two o'clock tomorrow; you will see that she writes. Now, please excuse me."

Ned pulled his cane free from its entanglement and made his way to his feet. Out of the side of her eye Kitty could see John Stanger's face, watching his friend with tension as if he wanted to help.

Ned took his leave of them and was gone, with a scrape and a clatter all through the hall. John Stanger sighed softly, perhaps not realizing Kitty could hear.

Feeling the awkwardness of the moment, for a second Kitty looked to Will, who could always be counted upon to fill an empty space with words. But he didn't oblige her. Instead he was staring at his plate.

"And if you will excuse me as well," said Mr Stanger. He nodded his head and took his leave politely.

"Will—" Kitty began, uncertain what she wanted to say.

Will raised his head. "Sorry, Kitty," he mouthed.

And then before she had a chance to protest, he too was off like a shot. And she found herself in the chilly saloon all alone.

She took a sip of her tepid tea and straightened her spine. Would the daughter of Katherine Wade Fairwell resent being deserted in such an ungentlemanly manner? No, Kitty told herself, she most certainly would not.

She turned to look at the brave parlour palm. Then she rose, and drew back the heavy curtains, flooding the room with golden early-evening light. Looking out, she leaned her head against the mullioned glass, trying to be heartened by the way the palm looked fresher already, and not disappointed by the way her imagined view had turned out to be nothing but an overgrown lawn reaching out to a dark and even more overgrown woodland.

"Well, my dear," she murmured to the palm, "I guess it's just you and me."

CHAPTER THREE

JOHN HAD NO NEED TO HURRY to catch Ned; he knew where he was going. What he didn't expect was the sound of brisk footsteps behind him.

Though, in retrospect, he shouldn't have been surprised.

He slowed, letting Will catch up with him.

"May I have a moment?"

"Of course, Mr Fairwell." Indeed, it was not only tolerable, it was something of a relief.

John had taken on the care of Ned and Gatewood House without hesitation or remorse—out of friendship, and in clear-headed recognizance that he would get a comfortable life, free from want, in exchange. He had no wish to give it up.

But sometimes he wished for someone he could talk to about troubled, asinine Ned Fairwell without betraying any confidences. He loved his friend, but he also often wanted to kick him in the teeth.

If there was anyone to whom he could confide, it was Will. He wrote to Will once a season, keeping him apprised of the business of the estate; and if he didn't include a line about Ned, Will would write back—damn the expense of the post!—and inquire.

In writing, though, John agonized over what to say. What could you say about a struggling man? "Some days good, some days bad." There were things John wouldn't commit to paper.

"Let us…" John took a step toward the door to the room that had once been a picture gallery, but was now his bedroom. Then he hesitated, feeling conscious of talking to a gentleman, even if it were only Will Fairwell. He couldn't vouch for the amount of mud and paperwork.

But no. He wasn't going to pretend to be anything he was not.

Besides, Will lived in bachelor rooms and was unlikely to cavil at untidiness.

He invited Will into the ridiculously still-called Italian room. Whatever had been Italian about it had gone on with the Eckerleys.

Will barely glanced around at the disarray before casting himself into one of the chairs at the small round table stuffed into the corner by the door.

John couldn't resent his comfort with the house. After all, it was, in everything but name, *his* house as much or more than it was Ned's. Ned didn't keep any secrets from John. So he understood the arrangements of the Fairwells better than Will might ever have imagined.

Yet even if he'd been inclined to resentment, which was not in his nature, it would have been hard to resent awkward little Will Fairwell anything.

He pulled out the other chair and slid into it.

"How is my brother?" Will asked. "He answers my letters but they are not…informative."

John thought. "He hasn't begged for laudanum since before Christmas."

Will swore, happily, and they shared a smile. When Will smiled he showed a hang tooth rather like a single fang.

"Less pain, then?"

"I don't know if his hip will ever stop hurting, what with shot and bone fragments still in there," John said frankly. "But as you can see he's better at getting around. It might be just practice—knowing exactly what motions hurt so he doesn't aggravate it as much. The scars on his face hardly bother him at all now."

"Thank God for small favours."

"And the headaches are less often—he'll still get one if he tries to read for too long, or if he's in bright light, but he can go longer."

Ned said he could still see a glimmer in the eye, and that was what made the headaches. John had suggested an eyepatch. "I prefer," Ned grumbled, "to look terrifying rather than mysterious."

But he did try an eyepatch, for a few days; the cord made a worse headache than the glimmer.

"How's his sleep now?" Will asked softly.

"And that's the best thing," said John, grinning. "You know how I told you I read him the Encyclopædia when he can't sleep?"

Will rolled his eyes. "I'm not going to forget anything as unlikely as my utterly unscholarly brother wanting to have the Encyclopædia read to him."

It was just a distraction. Will probably knew, but John wasn't going to explain.

In the beginning, Ned had sometimes needed to talk about the memories he couldn't help revisiting. But that wasn't always conducive to sleep—for either of them. They'd settled on the Encyclopædia when they couldn't think about the past anymore.

"It used to be twenty pages a night, at minimum. Now it's three or four—*or* I go in and he's already snoring. Your brother snores like an ox, but damn, it's an awfully nice sound when I've been with the tenants or in the fields all day and I want to go to bed."

"Ha! You're a good fellow, Mr Stanger."

John shrugged. "Well, it's not like I'm not paid for the pleasure."

"I suspect you'd do it regardless," said Will softly.

"Perhaps," said John. Probably he would have; he owed Ned. They'd been swapping debts back and forth for a while.

"Ah, and!" He smiled—he'd almost forgotten. "He's not so opposed to company as he was even a few months ago. The vicar called and he was *civil* to him."

Will snickered. "Of course, Mr Dunready is an eminently civilizing man."

"But not a bad chap for all *that*," tossed off John.

Then, after he'd said it, he worried that his humour might land astray. He knew from hard experience that gentry could get away with jokes he couldn't.

He shouldn't have worried. Will giggled.

"And of course," Will said, "there's the way he didn't swear at me and tell me to go to Jericho before I said a word."

"I wish I'd seen that," John said ruefully. By the time he'd arrived the argument had already been well on its way.

He looked at Will appraisingly. "You know you don't have to be afraid of him," he said carefully. "He thinks you're brilliant."

Will stared at him. "I'm sorry, he must have been talking about Robert."

"Neither of us is going to confuse the two of you," said John drily. "He meant you."

Will looked bewildered. "Oh. Well. That's nice. In the new sense, I mean, not the old. I don't believe it, but it's nice. I'm not afraid of him, as long as I don't look up. If I look up I remember he could squash me like a bug."

"My point is, he wouldn't."

"Yes, I know. I mean, I've known him my whole life. But he's bloody loud and huge and possibly you're tall enough that it doesn't bother you, but I'm a coward and I just deal with it by looking at my teacup. It's all right, don't worry."

Will seemed genuinely concerned that he *would* worry, but also confused why. John bit his teeth over a laugh. "All right."

"But he is looking well, and I'm glad. I know I have you to thank. You know that if you ever need anything, you can write to me."

John thought. He wasn't a schemer—if he ever had been, those days were long gone—but he was careful, and he knew to think before turning down an offer he knew was honest.

"Come visit more often," he said at last. "All appearances to the contrary, he likes it."

"I will," said Will, smiling again. "But for yourself?"

John leaned back and stretched out his legs with a sigh. Will could give him nothing but money. And he had enough money for himself, and his family, drapers in Leicester, were well-off enough that he didn't need to worry about them.

He had become inured to the world as it was and wouldn't seek, anymore, to make it different.

"Don't sell the place out from under us," he said.

Will looked shocked. "I *wouldn't.*"

John was amused to note how Will was sufficiently offended that he missed the pretence of it not being his decision.

"Well, then," he said, "I'm content."

Oh, why was that a lie? Why was it that the littlest thing—like disarrayed curls—could make him want the impossible?

He found Ned in his usual spot in the library, half-sitting, half-stretched out on his couch. Very near the fire, turned away from the room to face the corner. Ned liked to stay as warm as he could manage it, and the expense of coals wasn't a concern. Day or night, the library was usually hot enough to melt butter.

It was called the library, and indeed it had books in it, but Ned used the room as his bedroom and business-room as he couldn't manage the stairs to the second level.

The Eckerleys had taken the vast majority of their collection with them. All that remained from them were out-of-date *Highways and Byways*, books of unpleasant sermons, and multi-volume novels missing a volume. John had added books on agriculture and a handful of novels randomly purchased by post. And the Encyclopædia. Even then, it was not enough to fill the shelves, and the books slumped over.

The stocking of the library was one of the many things John had on his list to attend to. But it was a long list, and the fields and tenant business were more important. So, like many things pertaining to the estate about which Ned didn't care, it had gone by the wayside.

John took his usual daytime chair, the window to his side so he could read, but close enough to Ned's couch that he didn't have to strain his voice. The chair scraped around in the middle of the room depending on the time of day. In the long nights when the only light was the fire, he sat in the corner, baking, and holding the pages toward the flickering light as he read. There was no perfect spot, for him.

"So that's my sister," said Ned from behind his couch. John could see only his good eye and the top of his head.

"Why sound so grim when you say it?" said John. They had long ago passed the need for diplomacy. "She seems a little rash, certainly, but for a good reason. If you tell me she should have left her friend to a marriage with a batterer, then you're not the Ned Fairwell I know, and be damned to you."

Ned's silence was sulky. "But why bring her *here*?"

He was trying manfully not to whine, but John knew him better. He sighed, and made sure Ned heard it.

"Because she trusts you. And that girl needs time, anyone can see that. Just like you did. Just like I did."

Ned couldn't protest against that line of argument.

Instead he grumbled: "And with only a *maid*, not a proper chaperon. Her heart may be in the right place, but if the wrong rumour gets started, she might find that her precious *ton* doesn't care about what's in her heart."

"That's true. Do you think you can protect her from it?"

"Only by sending her back to Mrs Whalen as quickly as I possibly can."

John couldn't disagree. But there was an unsaid thing, and Ned had always trusted him to say the unsaid things when he couldn't. With his hands folded over his chest John said it, calmly.

"You wouldn't mind so much if Miss Green weren't so beautiful."

Ned swore at him, as was his wont.

Then, in a vanishingly small voice, he said, "You too?"

"Too skinny for me," said John briefly. "I don't fancy waifs. Even tall waifs."

Ned made an unhappy noise. There was silence, for a while. But

John had discovered, over time, that silence was a luxury he shouldn't permit Ned to hide behind. An argument was better.

"You could marry, you know," said John.

Ned actually laughed. "First I'd have to find a woman who doesn't flinch at the sight of me!"

"True. But there are a lot of women in the world."

"And one's as good as another, eh?"

"Well, no. *But* if you looked, you could find one."

"I'm sure that being rich would inspire a lot of strong stomachs," said Ned bitterly.

"Well, you would also have to do something about your personality."

Ned laughed again.

John said cheerfully: "Other than that, though…."

"Despite everything, my friend, you are an optimist."

"Relative to you," John said amiably.

"How's Molly Weaver?" Ned said, a dig at one of John's weak spots. "Is she taking you seriously?"

John felt himself redden, but with the back of the couch between them, Ned couldn't see. He dug around for some form of the truth he wouldn't get teased for. "I'm not sure I want her to."

"Good. *You* can do better."

Ned meant it as a compliment, but it hit John like a slap. Ned didn't realize what an unfair thing it was to say. Who was there, in a farming village of 200 souls, for a draper's son who worked as a steward? If the vicar had a grown daughter, perhaps—but the vicar was a baronet's third son; even he might have objected.

It seemed to John that he would always be caught twixt and between.

He said, "Thanks," and then took refuge in silence. As he'd counted on, Ned didn't notice.

"To be frank," Ned said at last, "I am surprised about Kitty. I remember her as a silly chit thinking only of dresses and being presented to the Queen."

Why did it bother John so much that Ned called her silly? What was it to him? He had no business having an opinion about his friend's sister's behaviour.

He just said, "It's been a while since you've seen her. She must have grown up."

Ned groaned. "Terrible thought. Soon she'll be stuck on some beau and wanting to get married. Oh, God. Can you keep them out of my hair tomorrow? If we talk, we'll quarrel."

"Kitty, or Will?"

"Both of them. He will take her side."

"He will take her side," John said gently, "because she is *right*."

Chapter Four

THE MARK ON LOUISA'S FACE was turning awful colours. Kitty made an attempt at coaxing her out of her room for breakfast, but she could hardly argue against Louisa's reasonable desire not to be seen. Louisa told her to go—that she herself only wanted to rest quietly.

Kitty left her in her maid Jane Addams's care after a brief discussion with Jane. Jane had the bad habit of speaking her mind, but Kitty could rarely bring herself to remonstrate with her, as they were often in agreement. Jane was fiercely prideful. Truth be told, Kitty preferred to know what she approved of and what she did not, rather than merely suffering poor work.

In this case, they were of like mind. When Jane said she would care for Louisa as if she were her own sister, Kitty knew she could trust her to stick to the commission with any care needful—up to and including a spot of fisticuffs to defend Louisa's good name.

Finally, rather later than she would have liked, she went down to the saloon. She met Will, but was disappointed to learn that Ned and Mr Stanger had come and gone already.

She made sure that a tray was sent up to Louisa, then ate in a hurry, absently gazing out the window at the overgrown back lawn. Will was writing a letter whilst finishing his tea, and grimacing most *horribly* over it.

"Who do you write to?" Kitty asked.

Will started with what seemed, surprisingly, to be guilt.

"Susannah, and father, and Mr Patel."

Kitty noted that there were already three letters folded and awaiting sealing. Will was working on a fourth. If Will hadn't been looking downright terrified she never would have noticed, but Will was the worst liar in the world. Why in heaven's name was he even *trying*?

Kitty was putting off her own looming task and welcomed a distraction. She smiled at him sweetly. "And?" she prompted.

Will reddened. "Tom Rutherford—since I'll be missing our whist game."

"How terribly disappointing." Kitty grinned at him. "You look as nervous as if you were writing to an *amour*."

Will scowled and pushed the letter in her direction. "See for yourself."

It was indeed as he had said, though he had barely written a single line beyond the salutation. *Dear Tom, I have got wrapped up in a scheme of Kitty's*

"Unfair!" Kitty sputtered. "A scheme?"

"That's what you get when you want to read other people's letters. Consider it a lesson to you."

Kitty huffed, but she was too amused to truly take offence. She drank her tea as slowly as possible, then finally gave in to the inevitable and returned to her room with slow feet.

Ordinarily, correspondence was a source of pleasure—but not so today. Her usual enthusiastic style, full of detail and exclamation, was severely dampened by not knowing how her news would be received. *She* was certain she had done the right thing—but Ned's words of censure preyed on her. How to convince others, without her being able to respond to their objections in the moment?

Her very first attempt was a false start. She crossed it out. She stared down at the page.

Surely dear, gallant Percy would understand! How dare she have this crisis of faith in his kindly nature? He had never done anything to deserve her doubt.

The difficulty was that she had a *little* more hesitation over the reaction of his sisters, the Misses Wolcott, and the letter had to be addressed to them.

Well—no, that wasn't quite true. She *could* write to Percy directly with full propriety. They had made promises, just the night before she'd left. She blushed down at the scratched-out letter. Even now she supposed that Percy's letter asking for her hand was on its way to Grandbourne! Her father certainly wouldn't reject his suit. The Wolcotts were *quite* respectable.

Of course, she knew her father well enough to realize that respectability was not the *first* thing he looked for. Patrick Fairwell, having been in love three times in his life (and having his heart broken three times—which gave Kitty a moment of torture), would first and foremost want assurance that the *affection* between the couple was sufficiently strong. Which Kitty would be able to assure him it was.

She had a bad shock realizing that her father would expect a letter from her, expressing this! In all her haste to rescue Louisa she'd forgotten!

"Oh, for shame, Kitty Fairwell!" she muttered to herself.

But now her conundrums multiplied. It did not at all seem right to send a doubled-up letter to her father containing difficult news (Louisa) and wonderful (Percy's asking for her hand). It seemed a bit beyond her.

But it would keep, wouldn't it? She was in the midst of an adventure! Her father was not himself a good correspondent; and Grandbourne was quite far off in Yorkshire; he wouldn't give a fig if her letter showed up a day or two later than it might have had she been more prompt.

She set it aside for the moment and once again attacked the letter to the Misses Wolcott with renewed zeal.

> My dearest Caroline and Mary,
>
> As you can see from the direction, I am writing this from my brother Ned's estate. Please accept my deepest apologies that I will have to miss tomorrow evening's musical interlude! Or I suppose by the time you receive this, it will be in the past—in any event I am very sorry.
>
> You are surely wondering what has taken me off so <u>dramatically.</u> It was an unavoidable circumstance, I believe!

She hesitated. Should she assume Bastable, or the Hargraves, had spread the story, and publicly slandered Louisa's name—or should she hope that Bastable had reconsidered his threat, and let the matter drop? If there were *not* rumours circulating, Kitty had no wish to start them inadvertently. But if there were, she felt Louisa deserved her strongest defence.

> I must warn you most strongly against the character of a man heretofore considered respectable enough even for the patronesses of Almack's. He is Mr Harry Bastable—the younger, that is. He has acted in a dastardly fashion.

Kitty was a little bit pleased that she had been able to use the word "dastardly." Her love of the Gothic had not *entirely* passed away.

> He seduced a young lady of our acquaintance and then <u>did her violence</u>. I have seen her bruises myself! I believe he ought to be punished most harshly

But of course, he wouldn't be—

> but as the young lady has no living male relations to ensure her safety, I had to take it upon myself to remove her from danger. I would never have imagined that <u>I</u> would ever have to take the role of the Good Samaritan!

The Misses Wolcott could hardly argue against the Bible! Kitty often attended St George's with them…although she couldn't help but feel they sometimes missed the point just a *trifle*.

> Yet of course we must do our best.
> I am as yet uncertain as to what I must do next, though I will do everything in my power to return to London <u>as soon as possible.</u>

After she wrote that, she hesitated. Why did it feel...not *quite* true? She was surprised. Why would she *not* feel eager to return to London—and to Percy's affection!—as soon as she could?

> Rest assured that you will be the first to know my plans!

On their own, the Misses Wolcott might be a little surprised at this assurance. They were friendly—friendly enough that they Christian-named each other—but they were not *bosom friends*. Of course, *Percy* would understand her meaning as a promise to him.

Oh, what *could* she say about Percy? Of course he would have told his sisters of his engagement. What could she say that was warm and yet still suitable for a shared letter?

> Please give my regards to your brother. It is with the warmest feelings that I look forward to very soon seeing you all.

Perhaps the underline under "all" was too much. Perhaps it wasn't enough. In any event—it was done.

Full of trepidation, she signed and sanded the letter. Then, before sealing it with wax, she took up a fresh sheet of paper and made a similar missive—with delicate amendments—to Mrs Whalen. A more passionate version went to the few girls she *did* consider her bosom friends—in Yorkshire, Mrs David Ivey (whom Kitty had known since childhood as Agatha) and in London, Lettie Price.

And then one final letter to her sister, Susannah—*now* pouring out all her feelings. Susannah had once been in a position even more awkward than Louisa's and Kitty was absolutely confident she would understand.

*

Having a fistful of sealed letters ready to be sent buoyed Kitty back to her usual confidence. She rapped gently on Louisa's door.

On entering, she found Louisa at the secretary looking pale. She, too, had been writing letters; her hands were inky and she was surrounded by far more false starts than Kitty had generated. Kitty had been wondering if Louisa might want her to look them over—perhaps her freshly-gained experience might have been useful?—but the two letters were sealed already, aligned sharply to the side of the writing surface.

"You must take heart," Kitty said; "Miss Horne has not raised you these last few years just to cast you off. You must give her credit."

"We will see," said Louisa in a flat voice, addressing the desk. "In any event, she knows the truth now. Miss Horne may consider me her duty. Lady Hargrave—I do not hope so much."

Kitty couldn't argue with that.

"If Lady Hargrave won't take you back…." she asked delicately.

"We gave up our cottage in Sussex when we moved in with Lady Hargrave. Miss Horne placed hopes that I would be married in my first season." She paused and then flatly uttered what she had never said out loud. "*All* her hopes."

"That seems, ah," Kitty paused, trying not to offend, then she gave up trying to find a word.

"Reasonable," said Louisa in a flat, angry voice. "I am, after all, the most beautiful girl of the season. If only I were better-behaved." Without looking up, she took the two letters, squared them in her hands, and offered them to Kitty. "Will you see that these are delivered?"

Kitty sighed. She took a step, leaned down and kissed the top of Louisa's head. Then she accepted the letters and took them downstairs for the footman to deliver to the post town.

*

From the staircase hall she could hear the faint sound of a voice from the saloon. She glanced through the door and discovered Mr Stanger speaking to Will. Mr Stanger caught sight of her in the doorway and smiled. He had such a pleasing, friendly smile! She returned it, blushing.

"Perhaps your sister would like to join us?" he said.

Will looked over his shoulder at her.

Kitty entered the room, mindful that her letters still needed handing-over. "Join you for what?"

"Mr Stanger and I were going to walk down to the village. I've never had a chance to meet the under-bailiff."

She was filled with relief. *Far* better to spend the day in the amiable company of Will and Mr Stanger than dwelling on Louisa's situation!

"Oh, I would like nothing more. Give me one moment—" She gestured with the letters. When they acquiesced she scampered off.

Tying the string of her bonnet beneath her chin she rattled back downstairs. Oh, *no*. She had to slow down and keep her dignity. Will had little interest in the requirements of ladylike behaviour, but what would Mr Stanger think of her? Twenty-four hours in the country and she was once again acting like a little heathen!

"I'm impressed," said Mr Stanger with a laughing voice, "a lady who says *one moment* and means it. You are scarcer than hen's teeth, I believe."

Kitty repented of her earlier self-criticism.

"I have a morbid fear of making a hen's tooth of myself," she said archly, "whatever *that* means."

They set off down the drive toward the village. Mr Stanger addressed Will regarding matters about which they must have corresponded. Kitty couldn't decide whether she was miffed at being left out of the conversation. She didn't *care* for farming. But that didn't mean she didn't understand it.

How many years of her life had she spent doing exactly this—trailing after her father as he tramped all across the estate talking to his tenants!

Through years and years she had dreamed and dreamed of the day of her coming-out, when she could enter a completely different world, not marked by muddy hems and freckled arms.

But she *had* trailed after him, because on those long walks—dusty or muddy—those were the only moments when she saw light in her father's eyes.

When they stood on the top of a hillock together and surveyed a field of golden wheat—Kitty hiding under her parasol and Patrick Fairwell decked in tattered clothes hardly finer than those of his tenants—he smiled and spoke to her in a low rapturous voice as if she, too, could see the beauty of it. And she could see the beauty of the wheat, in a way, but what she treasured far more was the beauty of his happiness. It was rarer than it should have been.

And that was, in part, her fault.

"Oh goodness, you're not arguing about enclosure again, are you?" she said with a groan. "Will, I thought you and papa had settled this a long time past?"

Mr Stanger raised his brow, looking at her as if surprised she was following the conversation.

"No argument *here*," said Will. "The Eckerleys enclosed as much land as they could long before we bought the place. It seemed to be more a matter of arse-backward principal in their case—'Render unto Caesar' and all that—"

Kitty's mouth twitched, but she didn't scold him for his language.

"—rather than making it more productive. Because they didn't seem to give a fig what they *did* with it once they'd fenced it off. Too busy bankrupting themselves with collecting art, I guess. The last steward was incompetent. But Mr Stanger has got *all* the fields on the four-course system now."

"The very last one has turnips now, instead of being fallow," said Mr Stanger with a sort of bashful pride.

"Very good, Mr Stanger," teased Kitty, "I look forward to your turnips."

"I can't take credit for the turnips," Mr Stanger demurred. "Your father has shared with me a treasure-trove of information about the latest agricultural methods—"

"Ha!" said Kitty. Of course.

"And John Tickle the under-bailiff does more than his share of the day-to-day work. I spend more time keeping the books in order."

"Your bookkeeping is *excellent*," said Will with the greatest satisfaction.

Kitty rolled her eyes. "Only you, Will, would say that as if it were worthy of a medal."

Will gave her a disappointed look. He was prone, at the slightest provocation, to lecture anyone who would listen on the importance of not being foolish with money. This had lost him a few friends, Kitty understood: living on credit and borrowing from friends to cover bad debts were the highest joys of the *ton*. No one liked a spoil-sport.

He opened his mouth; then closed it again. Kitty felt the sting of the rebuke, which had been omitted only because of Mr Stanger's presence, more deeply than had it been said aloud.

"I will take the compliment on my bookkeeping with pleasure," said Mr Stanger evenly; "as for what little knowledge I have otherwise, I can only thank your father and John Tickle."

Kitty tried to recover the lightness of the conversation. "Am I to take it that your passion for turnips arises from necessity and is not an inborn facet of your personality?"

Mr Stanger laughed. "Three years ago I wouldn't have known a turnip from a swede. My family are drapers, Miss Fairwell."

Kitty was taken aback. Except for a few of his vowels that

hinted at the Midlands, he sounded almost as Oxbridge as her brothers. She glanced at his neat blue coat, red waistcoat, and buff breeches; true, they were not a dandy's clothes, cut so tight they couldn't be put on without the help of a valet; but in the country he was unexceptionable. Indeed, he was far better dressed than Ned, who did not seem to acknowledge that it was necessary to wear cravats.

"Oh! I thought you were a gentleman. You were an officer with Ned, were you not?"

Unless he'd risen through the ranks, he would have had to buy a commission, which was more usual and what Kitty had assumed, given that he seemed to be only about Will's age.

He nodded slowly. "I was. The Crown accepts coin from the pockets of drapers just as well as from the pockets of gentlemen. In any event, it was a terrible waste of money—"

He stopped abruptly, checking himself as if he'd meant to say more, and chosen not to; Kitty was desperately curious to know why it had been a waste of money but she couldn't form a polite question to ask.

"I imagine the frame-breaking in Nottingham must have worried you," said Will.

Mr Stanger turned to him without appearing to notice the intentional change of topic.

"Of course. The Luddites may be dispersed or hanged, but matters are still unsettled. All I can say is, I am—at *this* point in my life—a practical man, and I am glad to be at Gatewood rather than in the cloth trade. Regardless of how the world shakes out, it is certain we will need corn and bookkeepers."

"We will need cloth, too," Kitty pointed out.

Having reached the village road, they passed the quaint stone church and a few small cottages, then turned down a path and finally neared John Tickle's cottage.

Shortly thereafter she found herself at a rough-hewn table drinking small beer (there was no tea) and listening to even *more* business about field rotation. She sighed to herself, uncertain what she was feeling. This reminded her of her girlhood, only—well, back then she would have had to force herself to keep a bright expression, for her father's sake; now, with no such burden on her, she found herself in an unexpected state of—contentment.

How ridiculous! These sort of country obsessions were precisely what she'd spent the last years trying to escape from. And she finally *had* made her escape, to be sure.

Percy's passions were sporting and horse-racing: he wasn't interested in the country beyond a keeping-place for pheasant and Thoroughbreds.

Surely, what she was feeling was only a silly kind of nostalgia—quite natural when one was faced with a permanent turn in life.

She kept glancing at Mr Stanger in search of his eyebrows. They were *present*, only hiding. She was amused every time she looked for them.

He was so different in looks from Percy—broad-shouldered, broad-jawed, dark-haired Percy. She wished Percy would smile more. That was his *only* flaw.

(But was that true? her brain pressed insistently. Certainly he was such a *good* man; there could be no arguing. But she didn't—she didn't—well. Perhaps she could *ask* him to smile more.)

Mr Stanger caught her looking for his eyebrows, and therefore raised them in a question; and the edge of his mouth lifted. Kitty blushed violently.

When the afternoon got on they headed back to Gatewood House. Kitty worried her bonnet strings with her fingers, unable to pin down why she was so disconcerted.

Mr Stanger fell into step beside her. "Have you enjoyed yourself today, Miss Fairwell?" he inquired. "This must be quite a step down after a season in London."

Kitty found herself saying, in a voice quite unlike her own,

"Well, that's true, but since I must be here, it was amusing enough."

"'Amusing enough'?" said Will, overhearing. "Oh, *lud*, Kitty, you sound as if you've been visiting too much with those Wolcott chits."

Kitty gasped. For a second she couldn't speak. Her voice rose. "Wolcott chits? What do you have against the Wolcotts? And *don't* say it's that they're spendthrifts. They've plenty of money enough to spend it on anything they like without *your* censorship."

"Well, they *are* spendthrifts," said Will, "but no, my objection is that they are completely inane, and when you say unKittylike things like 'amusing enough,' I have to fear it may be rubbing off on you."

Mr Stanger swallowed an utterance that may have been a laugh.

"You had better tell me what you mean by 'inane,'" Kitty said dangerously.

"Fatuous? Empty-headed? Interested only in trifles?"

"That's better than being only interested in *turnips*," Kitty snapped. "And if you'll pardon *me,* I find I have been amused *enough*."

CHAPTER FIVE

AFTER KITTY FAIRWELL STOMPED off in a dudgeon, John didn't expect to see her again for dinner. Which was a pity, because this was the first time in months he'd had an excuse to arrange for the cook to serve a proper meal. Ned didn't care what he ate, or when, so it often went by the by.

Nevertheless, Kitty Fairwell arrived on time, charmingly dressed in pale green silk with delicate lace trim. She had an expression that John couldn't define but it might have been either *glum* or *grim*.

She sat and drew in a breath. "I would like to beg pardon of you and my brother for my behaviour this afternoon."

Will Fairwell looked embarrassed. "No, no, you were quite right to stick up for your friends. Even if I don't like them, I shouldn't have insulted them. I'm terribly sorry."

Miss Fairwell blinked, and straightened, and wiggled. "Oh. Well, I—" she turned her pretty grey eyes on John. "I shouldn't have insulted your turnips, either. I did have a *lovely* time, and I thank you for taking me with you to meet John Tickle."

"My turnips can tolerate some insult, Miss Fairwell. Your presence was an improvement to the day and no apology is necessary."

John could clearly see Ned at the head of the table. Ned was sitting with his soup-spoon raised and his heavy black eyebrows stuck up as far as they would go.

"Do I dare ask?" said Ned.

"I was an arse and Kitty was rightfully mad at me," said Will.

Ned smiled slightly. "Oh?"

John hastened to change the subject. "Miss Fairwell, is your friend still not feeling well enough to join us?"

Miss Fairwell drooped. "She begs another day or two. Which is really too bad, for I had *hoped* she would come to church with us tomorrow."

"I can't *imagine* why she wouldn't want to listen to a sermon," said Ned. "With a giant slap-mark on her face, no less."

In lieu of saying "Oh, don't *you* be an arse," which is what he would have said if they'd been alone, John glared at him down the table. Ned shrugged and spooned up some asparagus soup.

John said, "*I* will come; I am not so against God or human company as your brother."

Miss Fairwell sighed. "Ned, *really....*"

Ned made a theatrical gesture with his wine glass. "I prayed to God and He ignored me. You can keep Him."

John rolled his eyes. Ned needed to be taken down a peg.

"You're just over-particular," he said. "*I* showed up, didn't I? And I'm not angelic, but I'll take it as an insult if you say 'halos required.'"

Miss Fairwell spoke up with a jest in her voice. "You know, possibly, if you had the sun behind you—and no hat—your hair *is* rather golden." She sketched a circle in the air representing his potential halo.

She had paused, regarding him with her lips parted. He thought for a second that she was going to ask why he wore his hair long instead of either cropped or curled.

Did he want her to ask? He did. But no, this was enough— the way she was looking at him in rapturous thought as if she were contemplating running her fingers through it.

Perhaps it was mutual, this attraction he had?

What a pity, if so.

The next morning, John again found himself walking down the drive to the village with Will Fairwell on one side and Miss Fairwell on the other. It was a miraculously pleasant thing, having educated people to talk to who weren't Ned.

Sometimes, if his path crossed the vicar's, John would fall in with him, but beyond him and his wife, the only denizens of the immediate area were the tenants, most of whom were illiterate.

All that trouble as a young man learning how to talk properly—and then no one to talk to. It was good that he had a wry appreciation for irony.

Of course, it often seemed that when Will Fairwell was your company, *you* hardly had to say a word. He was currently maundering about the recently-changed border of the parish.

Miss Fairwell came close to John, startling him. "Do be sure to *not* ask my brother why he didn't take orders," she murmured. "Unless you have a few hours."

John chuckled. "Yet now that you say it, I'm curious."

"It's *not* worth it, I *assure* you."

"Well, you know best."

The Fairwells attracted attention; John didn't know if the villagers *definitely* knew who they were, or if they were merely guessing, and being right.

John felt protective of the tenants and was therefore happy not to have the slightest shame about bringing the manor's owners to church: the Fairwells would *not* embarrass him. God knew there were *plenty* of landowners he wouldn't have been caught dead with in these circumstances.

The Colonel of his old unit, for one. One of the Majors…. There were two of the Captains whom John would still sometimes dream about punching in their over-fed faces.

Mr Dunready gave a respectable sermon about forgiveness; John didn't think that Miss Fairwell's friend would have quailed at it. Indeed, she might have found something to give her hope.

He slid his gaze sideways and saw Miss Fairwell listening attentively. She had wide lashy grey eyes that fixed intently upon her object of attention. For just this moment he was glad it was *not* him, because it gave him one moment in which he could admire her beautiful gaze whilst going unnoticed.

He pulled his attention away.

After the service was over John introduced the Fairwells to some of the tenants and other villagers who drew near in curiosity, and then to Mr and Mrs Dunready. Miss Fairwell thanked Mr Dunready with a glow on her face.

"It might well be a flaw of mine," she murmured to the vicar, "but I don't care for the sermons that are nothing but fire and brimstone. I go away feeling as if I can smell smoke on my clothes, but it never gives me the slightest feeling that I could do *better*."

Mr Dunready laughed out loud.

"How does one spend a Sunday afternoon at Gatewood House, Mr Stanger?" Miss Fairwell wanted to know.

"Arguing with your elder brother, in general, Miss Fairwell."

"Ah! In that case," she said decisively, "I will not feel too bad about asking if you'll show us the grounds. Behind the house, I mean, not on the village side."

"You will be most sorely disappointed," he warned her.

Will sighed. "Kitty, you should have given more thought to your own amusements when you lent me your book. Dank forest, or Mr Darcy? Can you wonder what I'm going to pick?"

"Oh for heaven's sake," Miss Fairwell said, laughing. "You *know* it will have a happy ending. Can't it wait for an hour?"

"It's already been waiting for *hours*," wailed Will.

"Very well; you can stay inside like the old maid you are. Jane and I will go, and I will see if Louisa will come out, and Mr Stanger will escort us—I am sure he will defend us—and besides, it is our own property! No one will assail us."

Will sighed. "I feel that this is something Sooze would scold me for. Or, worse yet, Mrs Whalen."

"Oh, come now, Will...."

Will smiled crookedly. "I know you'll be safe. Just do me a

favour and don't *tell* her."

"Your sister's honour and safety are quite safe with me, sir," said John solemnly. "I do not know Mrs Whalen but if Miss Fairwell has any complaint I am willing to stretch out my neck—" He mimed putting his head sideways and widening his eyes as if preparing for the guillotine.

Miss Fairwell shrieked with delightfully horrified laughter. John felt safe in grinning at her.

Will flapped his hand. "Go fetch your maid, then—and leave me to Miss Bennett."

"When we go back to town, I will find you your own Miss Bennett," said Miss Fairwell, "I promise."

"One thing at a time. First, a Mr Darcy for you."

Miss Fairwell blushed bright red and scampered off.

Feeling awkward, John took his leave of Will and went to enquire of Ned whether he wouldn't care to join them. But Ned's leg was plaguing him today and his response was unprintable.

John stayed in the library talking of nothing—no, indeed, of Miss Fairwell's remark to Mr Dunready about her clothes smelling of smoke, which was near enough to Ned's sense of humour that John thought it might make him laugh. Ned couldn't laugh just then, but he smiled tensely.

"There they are," said John, hearing, though the cracked library door, the clatter of shoes coming downstairs.

"Make sure she doesn't start dancing in a grove like a woodland spirit," said Ned.

John caught his breath uncomfortably.

"Is that likely?" he asked with care. Thank God Ned could be as dense as a bar of lead.

"I suppose not. She seems to have recovered from her infatuation with the Gothic."

John didn't say "too bad," but took a moment to thoroughly squash the mental image of Miss Fairwell dressed like a woodland spirit, dancing in the moonlight with her eyes half-closed—before going out to the hall to meet her.

He was relieved that Miss Fairwell's maid was joining them. Jane Addams was a tall, soft-cheeked girl with cutting eyes. Her prematurely greying brown hair was braided across her head in a crown. She nodded to him with silent dignity and then followed her mistress in the manner of a duchess in a queen's entourage. John felt suitably cowed.

Instead of leaving the house through the front, they passed through the saloon—where Will was already curled up on a couch with his nose in Kitty's book—and out through the French doors.

John guided the girls to the path. The lawn was shamefully overgrown—it had reached the height of his knees before lying down again under its own weight.

"This was supposed to be the back lawn," John said grimly.

He took them along the back of the house. "And this was, I believe, once a cutting garden."

The path curved; they followed it. A sea of thorns rose on their right.

"And this was a rose garden."

"Still is," contradicted Jane Addams mildly.

"Well, it's roses for sure; I don't know whether we should call it a *garden*." John sighed, and gestured them on.

It was a little bit of a walk up a gently sloping path before they came to the edge of the woodland. These were old trees left untouched when the manor had been built, not charming plantings added by a garden designer for romantic effect; the wood had the dank aspect of a fairy-tale involving a wolf.

The poorly-gravelled path separating the lawn from the wood was walkable only because John had had labourers out with scythes. The little dirt trails wandering into the wood itself were so overgrown as to be hardly identifiable.

Miss Fairwell, who had been silent as they'd drawn near, peered into the dimness of the trees and sighed. "I don't imagine there's a grotto in there somewhere?" she asked wistfully.

"Not that I've seen." He was aware that this was in part his fault. He tried to excuse himself somewhat, or at least explain. "For the first year we were here, I was—otherwise occupied. By the time I could attend to the grounds, they'd had too much time to go wild. I hired labourers to cut the edges of the path somewhat, so it doesn't rise up and swallow the house. But I don't know anything about this sort of thing. "

"Unless you are Hercules and this is an uncatalogued labor, you can hardly weed it by hand," said Miss Fairwell. "Ned owes you a team of gardeners, I think. Has he been a fool about it?"

"Ah, well—" John hesitated. "He thinks it not worth the trouble, as there's no one who will enjoy it."

"Oh, for heaven's sake! It wants taking care of. You oughtn't *have* a thing and not take care of it. It's like having a—a—a wife you don't kiss."

What on God's green earth had inspired her to use *that* analogy? John stared down at her, wide-eyed. Oh, the fierce, feeling expression on her face was going to keep him up at night.

"What a terrible thought," he managed.

CHAPTER SIX

WHEN KITTY WOKE THE NEXT morning, the weather had changed to a heavy grey damp. As consequence she felt it incumbent upon her to bring good cheer to the household.

She sorted through the clothes Jane had hastily packed and pleased to find that ever-wise Miss Addams had included her favourite sprigged muslin. Yet when she stared at herself in the mirror she discovered that it was still not quite *enough* to cancel out the gloom.

With her hair as yet undone, she went to see if Louisa had anything useful in her valise. Louisa gave her leave to make free of her crimson sash, which Kitty thought might be just the thing.

Jane, who had just helped Louisa dress, tied the sash beneath Kitty's bust, finishing it with a monstrous bow at the back. It took some minutes; Jane had an air of firm artistry that wouldn't permit an imperfect job. She pursed her lips, adjusting and re-tying. Kitty wiggled her feet.

"Stand *still*, Miss."

Kitty obeyed meekly. Then she dared tilt her head a little to address Louisa over her shoulder. "Will you join us for breakfast this morning? They ask about your health—Will and Mr Stanger, I mean; they really want to be *sure* you're well."

In the dressing-mirror in front of her, she could see Louisa sitting on the side of the bed.

"That is very kind of them," said Louisa tiredly. "I don't know what you ought to tell them. I am awaiting a stay of execution from Miss Horne and Lady Hargrave. Until that is settled I feel unfit for—" There was a long pause. "Being viewed."

"Keeping busy will distract you," Kitty said coaxingly.

She could see Louisa, in the mirror, making a face.

"How do *you* know, Kitty? You are always in such fine spirits."

Kitty flushed. "Not I. I mean—"

No, she hadn't told Louisa, had she?

In almost their first conversation, Kitty had asked about her relation to Lady Hargrave, and then discovered what they shared; they were being brought out by relations on account of being motherless. Louisa's parents had both died of fever four years ago, leaving her in Miss Horne's care. Kitty had apologized feelingly and Louisa, looking stiff and awkward, had said only, "Thank you." Kitty didn't gather they had been excessively affectionate.

So Louisa *knew* Kitty's mother had died bearing her, but as for the rest of it—Kitty had chosen not to touch on it.

But Louisa's comment required a response, and a truthful one would be of more use than a prevarication.

"What I mean to say," Kitty said, slowly but staunchly, "it's not *I* who's inclined to melancholia—but my father lost two wives and I fear he never recovered."

Two wives and—but, well, it wouldn't have mattered how long they'd been friends; Kitty wouldn't have told the rest of the truth.

Louisa hunched her shoulders. "Perhaps you are right. About keeping busy. But when I move, the bruises hurt, and it reminds me. Let me face one pain at a time. Will you return in the afternoon and tell me of your day?"

"Of course," Kitty said, and then, unblinking: "I was thinking of trying something different with my hair today; something like what you did at Mrs Van der Worst's ball. Will you advise?"

In the mirror behind her she saw Jane smirk. Kitty's scheme was not lost on her.

The problem was that whilst they both had a fashionable natural curl, Kitty had about twice as much hair on the whole. What had looked so excellent on Louisa at Mrs Van der Worst's ball required substantial—well, complete—reworking to sit well on Kitty.

With unusual clumsiness, Jane kept dropping the brush. She seemed incapable of following Louisa's directions, until Louisa at last huffed her way out of bed and took over.

"You're no help at all today, Jane," lied Kitty happily. "Go on, get yourself some breakfast."

Jane departed, grinning at Kitty behind Louisa's back, satisfied of a job well done.

After some struggle, the two young ladies achieved something that pleased both of them; Louisa even smiled and gave her approval, saying that the loose curls at the nape of the neck gave a Grecian air. To have a Grecian air, of course, was to be at the height of fashion.

Kitty hurried downstairs, aware of the potential irony that she might look particularly cheerful but show up too late for anyone to notice. But to her pleasure, when she arrived in the saloon, she discovered Will and Ned arguing in a desultory fashion about whether the latest news from the Continent could be trusted. Mr Stanger had finished his food and was gazing out at the rain with a faintly Romantic air.

After bidding her brothers good morning and fetching herself some food from the sideboard, Kitty sat next to Mr Stanger. "The change in weather will not do ill by your turnips, will it, Mr Stanger?" she murmured.

He looked at her and laughed. "My turnips are made of fiercer stuff, Miss Fairwell."

"And yet you have such a Byronic mien—as if the rain is the *Greatest Trouble in the WORLD*."

"I do believe Childe Harold considers gloom and rain a fitting background to his exploits." He looked rueful. "But, no, you see, it's far more mundane than that. I am making this cup of tea last as long as possible because as soon as it's done I have a five-mile ride ahead of me, along one of the worst paths in the parish. I have to go settle a dispute about a pig."

"By the time you ride five miles in the mud, and I presume five miles back, I fear you may be indistinguishable from the pig."

He raised his un-brows comically and made an up-and-down gesture with his palms in parallel. "A tall, skinny pig."

"Are you tall?" said Kitty cheerfully. "I hadn't noticed. Everyone is taller than me." Then she said "*OH!*" because something cold had just slithered down her neck. She smacked at it, but missed...because it dropped straight into her bosom. She yelped.

"Are you well?" Ned said from the head of the table.

Kitty was caught in the horror of not knowing how much Mr Stanger had seen. He had been looking *right at her*. But had he seen where the hairpin had gone? Or had he just seen her swatting herself madly like a ninny attacked by a spider? She shot a glance at him, but he was drinking tea. "I—ah—one of my hairpins misbehaved. I beg your pardon!"

The curl previously constrained by the hairpin now found itself constrained by nothing, and it flopped down against her chest.

Mr Stanger slid his eyes over to her and smiled over his teacup. Then he tipped it for the last drop and stood. "If you'll pardon me, gentleman; Miss Fairwell—"

After a brief pause in private to divest her neckline of the hairpin, Kitty wandered back to the saloon with a frown. She wanted to explore the inside of the house, but she wouldn't do so without Louisa. Yet she had to occupy herself in *some* interesting way, as, after all, she had promised to report to Louisa about her day.

It was good to have a goal in mind, but when she tried to fix on an activity her eyes kept roaming to the clock. The post wouldn't arrive for hours yet. This was the earliest day they could possibly expect a response from any of the letters they'd sent to London. Kitty had a queer feeling in her stomach when she thought about it. Of *course* she was sure of Percy, but—but she still wanted to see his assurance in writing. That was fair, wasn't it?

She wasn't at all sure she fancied the possibility of being scolded by him, even if he came around in the end. She would take being scolded by her father (when he bothered, it was important) or Will (because he was usually right, and endlessly forgiving); and Ned she could tell to go to Jericho; and Robert and Henry (oldest and youngest sons, inveterate heroes both) were more likely to *encourage* bad behaviour than the reverse. (Robert had brought his French mistress up to Grandbourne for Christmas one year, inexplicably. They had all behaved like proper *haut ton*, which was to say, they'd made jokes in French, lamented the Revolution, and shared recipes.) But she had a bad feeling that if Percy were to remonstrate with her she would take it…less well.

She just didn't like *not knowing*. That was all. She sympathized with Louisa's plight. If only the post would come!

"Will—" she began.

Will was upside-down on the saloon couch with his legs hooked over the arm and his book (or rather, her book) held over his face.

"Shush," he said.

Kitty got up with a huff. Now suddenly determined on a course of action, she rattled through the drawers of the sideboard. Then she marched out of the room.

"Who is it?" called Ned from inside the library.

"It's Kitty."

"Let yourself in."

Kitty did so. She surveyed the room. It was spare of furnishings, yet it still took her a second to identify the location of her brother. Then she saw his good eye looking at her with something less than gracious welcome over the swooping back of the couch tucked into the corner near the fire.

She resisted her first impulse, which was to squawk, "This lovely house and you don't spend all your time in the *corner*, do you?" but she realized in time that the answer was likely to be "yes."

She smiled, and settled on something else. "It's very snug in here. Is it comfortable for you?"

"As much as anything is."

"May I join you? Would you like to play something?" She held up the cards she'd liberated from the saloon. "Piquet?"

He groaned. "Oh God. No, I don't want to play piquet."

"You used to love piquet!"

"I used to. Now I lose track of the cards."

"Oh." She was taken aback. She hadn't seen him a great *many* times since his injuries but she hadn't noticed anything faulty about his memory. She didn't want to ask, but on the other hand, she had to. "Is it just cards or other things too?"

"Oh, don't look so blasted terrified. Sitting up for long enough to play cards makes my leg hurt. It distracts me."

"Ah! So if we play whilst you're on the couch, and I leave my tricks face-up, then it'll be a fair game. Or perhaps I can beat you *finally*. Being in London is good for one's skill at cards, you know!"

"I don't suppose you're going to take 'no' for an answer."

"I *would* understand if you wanted to play Hazard instead."

He didn't disappoint her; he muttered the Ned-like response of: "Better to lose at cards than win at dice."

She smiled. She investigated the space between his couch and the corner of the room. It was sufficient, as long as she didn't mind being warm. There was even a comfortable chair for her to sit on.

She hunted around the room, looking for a table low enough to lay out cards upon when playing with a reclining opponent. Finally she had to settle for another chair.

Ned squawked as she shoved it through the gap between head of couch and wall. She arranged it to her satisfaction, seated herself with her knees wedged up against the second chair.

There were no lights except for the fire—which was not six feet to her left—and the dim grey window-light across the room, which from her point of view was largely blocked off by Ned himself.

Ned had removed the unneeded lower cards and shuffled the remainder, apparently on top of his chest. He stretched out his hand

and offered them to her. She cut and showed the card. "Seven."

He shook his head. "You deal."

"My dear brother, I told you, I am positively a *masterful* piquet player these days. I no longer have to depend on the dealer's advantage!"

"But your reach is better," he said impatiently. "*Deal.* We can still trade off being elder and younger hands if it offends you."

Kitty shuffled again, dealt, and squinted at her cards, rearranging them in her hand. Ned, as non-dealer, was the elder hand and played first. He discarded the maximum five cards and replaced them from the *talon*—the eight remaining cards stacked on the seat of the chair. Kitty discarded three and took the final three cards of the *talon*. She kept her face composed, but she was pleased to draw the heart she needed, and indeed, the knave she'd hoped for.

"Point of five," said Ned.

Kitty had one card better with six cards; she could keep him from scoring. "Not good."

"Trio of aces."

"Good," she had to say. "*Oh.* I haven't anything to keep score with. Don't look at my cards."

"If you leave them over there, they will be safer than if they were behind Boney's lines."

Kitty squeezed out of her corner and rifled his desk in search of a scrap of paper and a pencil that was reasonably sharp. She hoped just a little that she would stumble across some excellent material for teasing—love letters? a memoir in progress?—but the correspondence that fell under her wandering eye was both boring and neatly organized.

She returned to the corner, marked down Ned's three points for the trio of aces, then another automatic point when he led the first trick with the king of spades.

"Point of six," she said for her six hearts. And her hearts were in sequence, so she collected the points for that too. "*Sixième* for sixteen—that's 22." She played the ace of spades, taking the trick.

"23. 24." She led the king of hearts.

"Either you're a better player than you used to be, or luckier," Ned grumbled.

"So you don't play cards with Mr Stanger, then?"

"No."

"How do you spend your days?" Kitty gestured with the pencil at the bookshelves, suggesting an answer.

"Staring at the wall."

Kitty sighed. "Evenings?"

"Letters. The Encyclopædia."

"What—do you mean?"

"Big book. Twenty volumes. Alphabetical—"

"I know what an encyclopædia is," Kitty cried in exasperation. "Do you mean to tell me that you spend *all* evening, *every* evening, reading the encyclopædia?"

"Not *all* and *every*. And it's John who reads."

Kitty had a momentary start at hearing Mr Stanger referred to as *John*.

She couldn't exactly scold her brother for occupying himself in such a harmless manner as reading the Encyclopædia, but still, it seemed like a half-truth.

"You never have company?"

"The vicar showed up once," Ned growled.

"*And?*"

"The second time, I wasn't at home."

"What about your neighbours?"

"Kitty, will you just *play*?"

She played and scored. "But what *about* your neighbours?"

"I don't think they've set foot on their own property in a decade. John knows their names; you should ask him."

She tried something—*anything* else. "Is Mr Stanger an educated man? He said he was a draper's son, but he doesn't sound it."

Ned laughed harshly. "You should ask him that, too."

"I won't; I'm afraid it might sound like an insult and I don't mean it that way."

"Smart girl," said Ned rudely.

"So I won't ask him. That's why I'm asking you."

"It's not my business to tell you about his life. He's friendly; he'll tell you."

"All right, I'll tell him you said so." She took a breath. "What's been your favourite article in the Encyclopædia?"

"My favourite *article?* Katherine Fairwell, don't treat me like I'm somebody's doddering uncle."

Kitty dug her heels in and put up a valiant fight at cards, but lost in the end. Ned seemed to think she had played well and didn't tease her, but still she couldn't bring herself to suggest a second game. Instead she escaped back to the saloon to wait, on edge, for the post to arrive.

When it finally arrived, Louisa still had no answer from either Miss Horne or Lady Hargrave, but there *were* letters for Kitty—and one of them was from *Percy Wolcott, Esq.*, not *Miss Caroline Wolcott!* With trembling fingers she swept it out of the grasp of the footman.

Unable to wait until she was settled into her own room, she took it straight away into the unoccupied dining room, right off the entrance hall, and stood by the window to read.

> Dear Miss Fairwell (if you will not think me too forward to address you privately),
>
> It was with relief that I heard your letter of the 24th. Already there had been rumours, not pertaining to you but to Miss Green and her entanglement with Harold Bastable. I am <u>very sorry</u> to hear they will not be married—my sisters say it is deeply unfortunate—but I insist to them that if you think it wrong it <u>must</u> be wrong. There is no one surpassing you in goodness & in that finest of qualities, Charity. Miss Green must know herself lucky to be your friend.
>
> I am so glad you are in the company of your brothers who can

advize you. I have written to your father but naturally over the distance I cannot expect a response so soon. I trust you will be delayed only a few more days at the outside.

I hope you are well,

Percy Wolcott, Esq.

Kitty sat in one of the chairs. She re-read the letter. It was perfectly all right. He understood. He had faith in her. She shouldn't have doubted him for an instant. It was very proper and—and— why was the word that came to mind "flat"? She reminded herself that some were better in person than in writing; Percy was *undeniably* one of those. She found herself becoming irritated with him, quite unfairly. After all, they were engaged—this was the first time he had written to her privately—couldn't he have taken the opportunity to put a little more, well, something into it? Why would you write to your fiancée and sign "I hope you are well"? "Yours fondly" would not have hurt, she was certain.

She opened the second letter, which was from Mrs Whalen. It contained a great deal of aggrieved scolding, but it was tolerably forgiving. Mrs Whalen had limited power over her; the worst she could do would be to refuse to sponsor Kitty's season, and Kitty was certain it would have taken more than this matter before she would threaten that.

She heard the sound of someone entering the house. Her lip trembled, but for what reason she couldn't say. Well, she had spent a long time with Ned, and he was excessively trying. Quickly she refolded the letter and tucked it into the bodice of her dress.

It was indeed Mr Stanger in the hall. She gave him a nod of greeting, admired his impressive quantity of mud, and passed upstairs to keep her promise to Louisa.

Well, perhaps she wouldn't tell her quite *everything*. Louisa didn't know about her engagement to Percy—it had just happened, after all! and it seemed so hurtful to rub her friend's face in her own success. It would keep a while, until it could be officially settled.

CHAPTER SEVEN

"YOU KNOW, I DO BELIEVE he is in love," said Kitty. "There's no other explanation for it."

"Why do you say that?" asked Louisa.

"Well, usually I can count on Will to talk the ears off maize, but he keeps falling quiet. He *claims* to be reading a novel, and I think that's true, but I went into the room earlier he was just staring at the ceiling—and then when he saw me he got the guiltiest look and snatched the book up again. It's so unlike him. So you see why I say it!"

"Whom do you believe he loves?"

"Well..." This was a sticking point in Kitty's theory. She said doubtfully: "Mrs Whalen's ward Mary Fettinger has set her cap for him. But I can't imagine it is her. He makes such pitiful eyes at me when Miss Fettinger is after him. He is so grateful to be extricated; I am always amused."

Louisa chuckled a little. "You are a rescuer extraordinaire."

"I try to—I try to do my best." Kitty sighed, her shoulders falling. "I seem to fail with Ned."

In relating the game of piquet to Louisa, she had skimmed over the details. Still, she had conveyed the gist.

"Perhaps his troubles are beyond your touch. There's no shame in that."

"I suppose," Kitty said sadly. "I suppose. In that case, thank God for Mr Stanger! Yes, for both things. He cares for Ned like a brother, with such loyalty. And yet he is so gracious to Will and me. His conversation makes meals—" she was almost going to say "tolerable," but stopped herself. "Tolerable" would make Louisa feel Kitty was suffering here, and, Kitty was surprised to discover, it was not so. "Awfully pleasant. And he would never say a word against you, nor let anyone else do so in his presence. It is almost as if he is our host, and Ned the sort of—ghost in the castle. You feel him like a waft of cold air in the corridor but you see only a flicker. Good heavens, that's terrible, isn't it? And about my own brother, too!"

"You ought to write novels, Kitty; but you are too kind to do it well."

Kitty laughed.

"What does Mr Stanger speak of?"

"Oh, all sorts of things! He could make you love this place, even despite—Ned's cold draught. But I don't know what else a bachelor would do here besides read; Ned keeps out of society and Mr Stanger says he doesn't care for it either."

"Surely he must want a wife."

It struck Kitty for the first time to consider whether Mr Stanger and Ned were more than friends. In her family this was not a shocking line of thought for a young lady, given, if even *nothing* else, that Ned's twin sister Julia was an avowed Sapphist. But no, she knew Ned liked women, even if he'd never had any luck with them.

And as for Mr Stanger, there was something—well, there was something about the way—when her hair had been tumbling out of ill-placed pins that morning—he had looked at her, without answering her apology, with a smile over his teacup. And then he'd quite mildly excused himself. At the time it had made her feel—as if he'd touched her curls, featherlight, and then taken his hand away. It had made her blush then, unsettled in body and mind, and it made her blush again now. She turned her face away from Louisa and took a turn around the room.

"He probably *does* want a wife, but more fool him for falling in with Ned, instead! Ned hasn't a romantic spot of warmth in his soul. He probably put something dreadful in the steward's contract like—'You *must* reside on the premises. Ladies may visit only between four and five o'clock on Wednesdays, and *women of lower breeding*, NEVER. Fatherhood is *GROUNDS FOR IMMEDIATE DISMISSAL*—'"

Louisa put her hands over her face, stifling laughter. "Oh, Kitty. He might need rescuing, too."

Kitty shook her head briskly. "No, no, he's a grown man. If he lets Ned treat him unfairly, that's his problem."

"I dare you to ask him."

"Which? Ned, or Mr Stanger?"

"Either."

"If the circumstance arises!" Kitty said.

But it didn't, for despite sitting next to Mr Stanger at dinner she spent the whole meal encouraging Will to share his knowledge of tactics in whist, piquet, and loo. Not that it required much *encouragement*.

To her great triumph, she secured Louisa's promise to explore the house with her in the morning. All Kitty had to do was make sure they would be left alone. And with such a small and predictable household, that was easily enough done.

Kitty had confirmed over dinner that the business of the pig was *not* settled, so Mr Stanger would be out in the mud again, poor soul!; Ned of course would be sulking in the library; and as for Will, it was easy enough to drop a word in his ear and request that he read *P&P* in his own bedchamber.

The two young ladies shared breakfast upstairs and then they waited until they heard Mr Stanger go out. Louisa had some good colour in her cheeks for once.

They first whispered downstairs to the saloon. Kitty went ahead to confirm that Will had followed her request; he had. She and Louisa took a turn around the room, lamenting the discordancies and mentally filling in the omissions.

"I've been calling him Rudolph," Kitty commented about the parlour palm.

"Why Rudolph?"

"I don't know."

Louisa gave her a puzzled expression. Kitty supposed that was only fair.

Through one of the doors leading off the saloon, they discovered a music-room, painted a cheery pink. It was clearly a music-room as it contained a piano tucked against the wall, though absolutely nothing else—not even curtains or carpet.

"Perhaps it was too awkward to be thought worth moving?" Kitty wondered.

Louisa gravitated toward it. She didn't sit, but she did raise the lid. Her hand hovered over the keys.

Still, she hesitated.

"Oh, please go on!" Kitty exclaimed. "If you don't, I will."

Louisa tilted her head. "I've never heard you play."

"There's a reason!" Kitty said cheerfully.

Louisa played a chord, then another.

"Oh, it's in tune," murmured Kitty, pleased.

Louisa made a run from the high notes down, slowly but with some competence; one of the lower notes went *AANG*. She winced but went on, discovering only one other misplaced note. She withdrew her hands and closed the lid once again.

"It isn't my skill. Usually it's Miss Horne who plays, whilst I sing."

"And beautifully, too. You have such a wonderful voice. Will you sing something?"

"No," Louisa said at once, too abruptly. "Oh, I'm sorry, Kitty. Not now." She turned back a little to look at her friend halfway, in that shy way she had. "It's as if it takes so much of my soul, and I don't have it to spare."

Kitty went to her, took her hand and pressed it affectionately.

"When I hear you sing, it will please me so very much, because not only will I have the pleasure of your voice, but I will know you are feeling yourself again."

"That is something for me to look forward to, as well," Louisa said softly. "Let's go on. What's through that door?"

Kitty crossed the room and tried the second door, but it was locked. "Oh! That must be the other room that connects to the library, I think. Perhaps that's where Ned keeps the shrine to his horribly murdered first love."

"*What?*" cried Louisa.

Kitty couldn't keep a straight face and she was already laughing. Louisa stared at her for a second and then started to giggle, covering her face with her hand.

"Oh, your face!" Kitty howled.

"You are so dreadful!" said Louisa between giggles. When she controlled herself, she was able to ask, "Was he ever married?"

"Good heavens, no!" Kitty felt she had exclaimed so quickly she had been unfair. She hastened to clarify. "Even before his—ah—he was never *charming*. Sweet, sometimes," she added quickly. "Kind. Not charming."

Still laughing, they traipsed back through the saloon. The other door led into another unfurnished room. This one had walls the colour of spring grass.

"I would make this a withdrawing room," Kitty mused. "Perhaps it was."

Louisa tried the next door, which opened. On the other side they found walls papered with a small feminine pattern of pink, blue, and green flowers. A deep, tall, old-fashioned desk loomed large against one wall. Yellowed and dismaying lace drooped from the window.

"A lady's boudoir," declared Louisa. "She kept her correspondence there at the desk, you see—but she wanted something more stylish so it was left behind."

Kitty quite agreed.

They tried all the drawers in the desk but each one opened without needing a key. Kitty measured carefully to make sure they hadn't missed a secret compartment. Finally she decided it was impossible.

"Let's see the wing that was supposed to be a portrait gallery. I'm dreadfully curious."

"*That* wing—but not the other?"

"Not unless you want to tangle with Ned. You can only get to it through the library and that's *his* haunt."

"I'd rather not," Louisa said hastily.

"He makes that section of the house so wonderfully Gothic," said Kitty with satisfaction. "I'll have to remember to tell him so tonight over dinner."

They went to the dining room at the front of the house and opened the door at the far end. This was the moment Kitty had been waiting for, and she wasn't disappointed.

The gallery wing was not palatial, but still, for a house of this size it was impressive.

There were no portraits in the portrait gallery—true. There was no carpet, nor paint or trim, and the ceiling hadn't been fully finished on the inside. But it was full of something even better— both more Gothic, more unexpected, and more useful. Furniture, draped in dusty white cloths!

"Good heavens!" Kitty crowed. "It's been here all along! Will you help me decide where to put it?"

"Won't your brother mind? It *is* his house."

"He's got an empty music-room, drawing-room, and boudoir, and who even knows what we'll find upstairs. Look at this dust." Kitty held up a coated finger. "We can put it all where it belongs and if we close the doors afterward *he may not even notice for months.* By which time we won't be here. Why would I pass up this opportunity for completely harmless mischief?"

"Why haven't the servants done it?"

"They probably made the mistake of asking permission."

"Why hasn't Mr Stanger done it, then?"

"A very good question. I will ask him. *After* I've fixed it the way I like it. Are you going to worry yourself out of the best fun?"

Louisa was lifting up a sheet with two hands, examining with pleasure a music stand with a harp-shaped back. "Not at all. Kitty, let's start with the music room!"

There would inevitably be a point at which they'd have to find one of the footmen to help move the larger pieces, but first they began with an inventory. They folded up the sheets with as little to-do as possible, trying to keep the dust low.

Together they tallied four cabinets of varying sorts—three desks —five small tables—two medium-to-large tables. One green baize faro table, with cards pasted around the edge to mark the bets (Kitty sniffed; the players' odds were good in faro but it required so little skill). Three fancy chairs, and more plain chairs than any household could ever require, though they were all disreputably mismatched. Only two rugs—most disappointing. One trundle bed, without mattress. A cracked mirror, which Kitty promptly covered back up. ("*Too* Gothic!") Several spare chamberpots. A short *thing* with a hole in its back and four delicate legs ending in paws.

"I can't imagine what it *is*," Louisa said.

"Oh! I think it's a plant-box. To go under a window."

"We should get a mate for Rudolph!"

Piece by piece, *almost* on tiptoe, they transferred the music stand, a small table, and three chairs to the music-room, which was at the farthest corner of the ground floor.

The door to the library was directly across from that of the dining room, so if Ned were being attentive he could catch them quite easily. They watched it nervously, but it stayed closed.

When they *were* caught, it was the butler, Howard, appearing from nowhere. He met Kitty in the staircase hall as she took across the fourth and last chair.

Howard said not a word. He simply stood with his arms crossed, and raised an eyebrow at her. He was as pale and gleam-ingly bald as a marble senator.

Kitty gave him her beamingest smile. "Might we have some

rags, Howard? It was all covered well, but there's still a bit of dust."

He had the utmost mastery of that most necessary of butlerial skills: imperturbability.

"Yes, Miss Fairwell. Are you in need of assistance?"

"For the larger pieces, later—but at the moment we're still *planning*."

"Yes, Miss Fairwell."

As they shuffled the chairs into matching sets in the portrait gallery, Louisa discovered a chest that had previously been hidden. She pointed it out to Kitty, who at once sidled behind the line of chairs in order to investigate.

"It's not locked! Oh, it's old clothes! Silk, too!"

"Can you pass them out to me?"

They had enough difficulty removing just the first dress. It was old-fashioned, with a slim bodice and very full skirt. It might once have been pale brown or perhaps apricot but was now faded. Kitty held it up; it looked to be about her size.

"It must be from the '90's, don't you think? My mother might have worn a gown like this. Look at how lovely the lace is."

Louisa was delighted at the discovery, and that pleased Kitty more than anything. She didn't have the idea that Louisa had ever had much chance in her life to fool around and play dress-up.

"Does it fit?' Louisa asked. "If it fits, you'll have to wear it to a masquerade ball!"

Kitty poked at the fastenings. "Shall I find out?"

It took the both of them to get her into it, working out the layers of petticoats that they hauled out of the chest. Kitty's hairdo was a victim of the affair. She untangled it with her fingers, letting her hairpins slide away.

"How do I look?"

"Oh, like a fairy! I'll uncover the mirror so you can see."

"No, it's bad luck; let's use the one in the hall."

*

They ran into Will in the hall, as well as the footman, coming in with the post and the newspaper. The footman bowed and left.

"Ah, sorry," said Will absently to Kitty and Louisa, "I'll be off again, I've just come for the post and a bite to eat."

Louisa was frozen rigid, not at coming across Will unexpectedly, but because he had the post in his hand. He was peering at it.

"That's for me," she said in a voice devoid of feeling. "That one. From Miss Horne."

Kitty's stomach sank; she felt unsteady.

Will gave Louisa a kind, worried look with his brows pulled together. He extended the letter somewhat hesitantly, as if wishing he had some *sal volatile* to go with it. "Yes. Ah, you know, Miss Green, the light's better in the saloon, if you want privacy...."

Louisa had already snatched it from his hand and snapped the seal open. Her face was completely without colour.

Kitty and Will both waited in silence for the brief moment it took her to read the letter.

"Bastable has said exactly as he threatened," Louisa said flatly. "Lady Hargrave has washed her hands of us. Miss Horne will fetch me."

"Is that all?" Kitty tried.

"She does not mince words."

Kitty caught her elbow. "Listen, Louisa! I don't know what your income is without Lady Hargrave, but if you need help—" Across Louisa's shoulder she gave Will a dig with her eyes daring him to contradict her; but of course Will had a soft spot the size of America. He looked as fierce as if he would have said the same, if she hadn't.

"If Miss Horne and I combine our means, we can make do," said Louisa in a shaking voice. "Thank you. No, I would like to be alone. Thank you, Kitty. Mr Fairwell."

She made her way to the stairs with such speed as to be almost a run.

"What a bad business," Will said doubtfully. And then, frowning at Kitty as he focused on her for the first time, his eyes widened. "Where the deuce did you get *that?* By God."

Kitty wasn't thinking about the dress. "In a chest—I imagine it was left by the Eckerleys. Or ought I sent back to them?"

"No, Kitty," Will said helplessly. "It's yours; I mean, it really is yours, by right. It was our mother's."

Kitty looked down at the dress. She didn't seem to be taking this in quite right. "What? Whose mother's?"

"Ours. Katherine Fairwell."

"But why's it here?" she asked stupidly.

"We found the chest in storage at Grandbourne and father— didn't want it around to remind him. We had just bought Gatewood and were sending some furniture here, so I put that in with the rest. And I forgot about it at once."

"Oh," said Kitty, still feeling mushy-brained. "She was just my size."

"And your colouring, too, from what I remember. It's a pity they all had powdered hair in the blasted portraits."

"Ought I take it off?"

"Of course not, it's yours; have it made over for yourself if you want—if the lace won't fall apart. But just wear it in London, eh? Not at home."

Kitty nodded, speechless.

Will sized up her expression. "Here, come and have a bite with me—it's still hours till dinner. Hm. And perhaps a little brandy."

In that careful, should-have-been-a-vicar way of his, he made sure that one of the meat pies, a pot of tea, and a small glass of brandy were sent up to Miss Green's room. He and Kitty shared the remainder.

Kitty ate with tremulous care, terrified to spill something on the dress. She couldn't change out of it on her own. She could ring for Jane, but Jane wouldn't expect her for the dinner change for some time; she would *eventually* show up, but she would be cranky. Putting it off was, at this moment, more tolerable.

Finally Kitty finished the meat pie and the brandy and didn't care quite so much about changing out of the dress, a magical trick she had previously observed of brandy.

Will was reading the paper.

"Oh *hell*," he said, in a very short, serious way, about something he'd read in the paper.

They had two brothers still at war. There was no amount of brandy in the world that would have kept Kitty from gasping in horror upon hearing a tone like that. "*What?*"

"No, no, no, it's all right. I mean, it's not. But it's not like *that*."

Kitty demanded to know; he refused to explain; she accused him of being in the midst of an intrigue; he blushed furiously; she shouted "AH HA!"; he tried to hush her; she tried to get the paper away from him to establish what the connection was; he scrambled up the pages to disguise his place and she stared at column upon column of fly-speck type in dismay.

Finally she just said: "But it's *not* all right, and you could help?"

He stared at her. "Ah, er, I don't know. Perhaps. Not here. In London."

He got sort of a hang-dog look: but he would never ask.

Kitty straightened out the situation for him, in short words.

After a couple of rounds he said meekly: "I won't go if you don't *wish* me to." (She assuredly had the upper hand.)

"It hardly matters. Miss Horne will take Louisa back to London in a day or two and I will go with them." Or if their plans were less amenable, she would rearrange them to her own liking. "There's no point in you *also* lingering around here heartbroken."

He saw her point, and thanked her profusely. "If I leave now, I should be able to make London before dark without having to stop the night anywhere."

Kitty thought it was wishful thinking, but merely begged him to take care.

"But!" she added, "you mayn't take *Pride and Prejudice*; get your own! Jane's just started it, and then I intend to give it to Louisa."

Will gave her a kiss. "But are you *sure*? If you need anything, insist that Ned—ah, you may as well go through Mr Stanger."

Kitty smiled. "I do believe you are quite right."

Will was off within the hour. Kitty heard a bit of shouting from the library, but if Will's course were set, Ned wouldn't be able to dissuade him. She had no fear.

She wandered up and down the portrait gallery again, but it looked gloomy now, and she shivered to be there alone. Besides, she had discovered a suspicious drip-stain down the farthest wall and that worried her. She repaired posthaste to the saloon, where there was a cheerful fire.

There was also a mirror. She stopped and looked at herself full view in her mother's dress for the first time.

She didn't know what she felt. She had some of her mother's things—a locket, a portable writing-desk, jewellery that was too grand for an unmarried woman to wear: she wasn't wanting for mementos. Mementos, yes, but she had not a single memory; her mother hadn't survived Kitty's birth beyond a few hours.

Thinking about it like that always made Kitty's head foggy. She wished she could just grieve, and *miss* her mother, like everyone else did—but she felt the agonizing pain of being an accidental murderess. Of course it wasn't her *fault*, she was perfectly sensible of that. But it was *because* of her that her father had once again been devastated, and her brothers and sisters had lost their mother (either *actual*, in the case of Will and Henry, or warmly accepted, in the case of the others).

Wearing her dress—it was so strange. If she'd known whose it was, would she have put it on?

She felt her own name suited her, but at the same time she wished it had been *different* from her mother's. And she liked her looks, but those were her mother's too. There were many moments when her father glanced at her with sudden sadness and she wished that she were tall and dark and black-haired like Julia or Susannah. Just to not be a *reminder*.

She curtseyed to herself in the mirror, as she'd done when practicing before being presented to the Queen.

"Kitty Fairwell," she murmured, introducing herself.

No, her name would not be Fairwell for much longer.

"Kitty Wolcott."

A perfectly fine name. But when she was a married woman she might prefer:

"Katherine Wolcott."

How grand it seemed! She went on.

"Katherine Fairwell."

No, when her mother had worn this dress she had probably been a Wade, not yet a Fairwell.

"Katherine Wade. Kitty Wade."

Someone knocked on the wall by the open doorway. John Stanger's voice inquired, "Who is the lucky Mr Wade? Or is he a Lord Wade?"

Chapter Eight

Miss Fairwell turned with a smile.

"No, no, Wade was my mother's family name. This was her dress. A chest of her things ended up here amongst the furniture."

He knew he shouldn't have been so absolutely delighted to hear that there was no Lord Wade in the wings.

He looked at the dress, which happened to mean that he had a fair opportunity to look Miss Fairwell up and down without it seeming ill-mannered. His family sold cloth for all purposes, leaving the *fashion* of it to tailors and modistes; but he did have sisters, and the cloth business was a good one to do well in. They dressed quite as fine as any *haut ton* ladies.

After five years in His Majesty's Army and two years at Gatewood House, his inadvertently-acquired knowledge was rather out of date. Still, he could recognize that the dress, firstly, was decades out of style, and secondly that it looked *very very good* on Miss Fairwell.

Modern dresses were fine and thin and left little to the imagination, but they were also oddly ignorant of the concept of a slender waist such as one might, for example, want to tuck one's arms around. This dress snugged in just in the right place.

"The bow suits you," he managed.

She looked down at her chest. "Yes, it's sort of dreadfully silly, isn't it?" she said with good cheer.

He paused, then said wryly, "I'm sure there's something diplomatic a gentleman would say to that—but my boots are muddy."

She grinned. "Fairly said, Mr Stanger! Did you get the pig sorted out?"

He was able to accept, from seeing her chatting with John

Tickle the other day, that she wasn't making fun of him. Landowners ran the whole gamut from "personally sorting out pigs" to "haven't set foot on the estate in a decade" (the Duke of Devonshire was famous for that). From the spots of correspondence he'd had with her father, he knew Patrick Fairwell, at least, fell quite on the former side.

Some families were filthy rich. The Fairwells seemed to be *quite* rich but also *not infrequently* filthy at the same time.

"The pig was turned to bacon a while back. The *pig* wasn't the problem."

"Oh *dear*."

He sighed. "It's settled."

He had permission from Ned to fix all problems costing less than 5*l.*—which was quite a bit more than the value of the pig—but getting the two men claiming ownership of the pig to come to an agreement they both thought tolerable—which was to say equally unfair—had taken up more of his life than he would have liked.

Miss Fairwell probably would have followed if he'd explained, but he was rather done with the topic for the day.

"Now that you have the dress, will you repatriate it?"

She looked down at herself. Her fingers plucked the lace of the skirt. "No-o-o," she said slowly. "I will leave it here. It's beautiful, but at the same time it…makes me sad."

John hesitated. "I'm sorry about your mother."

"It's not as if I knew her, Mr Stanger," she said stiffly. "Never mind."

He almost said, "I hardly knew my daughter, either, but that doesn't mean I don't think about her every day." But she'd said "Never mind," and not knowing how much Ned had conveyed to his family about John's own history, he wasn't sure *he* wanted to explain either. So he left it alone.

Miss Fairwell raised her face, frowning severely, and struck off hard in another direction. "Now, listen, Mr Stanger! You must talk to Ned about this place. It's going to fall down around your ears."

Unlike my heart, he thought, which has fallen down around my feet.

Well, hell, he thought.

Well. It was all right. She'd be gone in a few days.

On the obvious assumption that he would follow, she swept across the ground floor to the dining room—lighting a candelabrum on the way—and then cast open the long-closed door to the would-have-been portrait gallery. John was somehow unsurprised at her familiarity with it.

He took the candelabrum in order to hold it up. The sun wouldn't set for hours but the gallery was crowded and had many dim corners. He surveyed the room. The dust cloths were folded neatly on top of the largest of the tables.

"Did the servants help you?" he asked.

"We didn't get that far."

"You and Miss Green?"

"Yes. Really, Mr Stanger, you've got almost a whole household in here! Why didn't you set everything out?"

"Because it's just the two of us," he said, a bit shortly. He would have rather done the house up properly, too, but there were good reasons why not. "Ned doesn't keep enough servants to keep the whole house clean, if it's furnished. We're already a bit short-handed and I don't see any point in giving them more work than necessary."

Miss Fairwell sighed. "Of all my family, *he's* the one who's picked up Will's pinchpenny ways. I do apologize. Mr Stanger, tell him to hire another—no, *two* more housemaids. I will be visiting again in the near future and I expect my brother to be living in decent surroundings."

Visiting again in the near future? thought John. Oh, that's bad. Good. Bad. One of those things.

"And next time I visit, I will also be having the vicar and his wife to dine. And I will take them on a *tour*. How about that?"

"He isn't going to like it."

"If he complains about the expense, tell him that I am more than willing to pay the girls' salaries out of my pin money. *And* the servant tax."

Ned was fairly impervious to shame—about things like that, in any event. "He'll tell you to go right ahead."

"Make sure one of the girls is a good seamstress," said Kitty bullishly, "because some of the rooms want curtains. Would you mind sending an order to your family?"

John had to laugh. "Well, as long as I can tell him it's all your idea—whilst I'm at it, there's the matter of the walls in what I think used to be Mrs Eckerley's room—and the flooring in the withdrawing room, I don't know if you saw it—and some of the windows upstairs need new panes. The butler and the housekeeper have been begging." They had pride, even if Ned didn't.

"Make a list and I will back you up. Next time I come by we can tackle the wings. *Oh.* But come over here!"

She took him firmly by the arm that wasn't occupied with the candelabrum. He was glad he had a healthy heart or he wasn't sure he would have survived. But he had no time to think about it, for she was tugging him around the edge of the room to what *had* to be the darkest corner. He had no choice but to fully occupy himself in not running into stray furniture, on the one hand, or stepping on her full skirt, on the other.

"Slow down—mind the candles," he begged.

With some effort they made it around to the wall farthest from the door.

"Hold the light up," she demanded. Her white hand flashed upwards through the light. "There. Look at that!"

John held the candelabrum as close to the wall as he dared; then he couldn't fail to miss what she was pointing at. "*Damn*," he said. "Er. Pardon." He freed himself from her grasp and felt the wall. To his relief, whilst there was a long trickling stain, it wasn't currently damp. And it *had* been raining; so there must be some sort of reservoir on the roof that only overflowed intermittently. He stuck his nose against the stain and sniffed. A slight off smell, but no mould. Thank God for small favours. He lowered the candelabrum.

"I am embarrassingly reminded that I am but a journeyman at this estate-steward business," he said glumly.

"*This* is why you need more servants. Because they would have *noticed*. You can't expect to take care of the corn *and* the tenants *and* the house *and* the bookkeeping *and* read the Encyclopædia to my sulky—"

John raised his eyebrows. So Ned had told her about that, had he?

"—arse of a brother."

"Miss Fairwell!" he managed.

"Oh, don't be shocked, Mr Stanger. I have three brothers in the Army, I can identify and name an arse when I see one. Are you going to tell on me?" She sounded entirely confident he would not.

"Of course not."

"Does Ned do *anything*?" she demanded.

"The correspondence," John said meekly, although often enough Ned would only answer the post after John asked about it repeatedly.

"Considering how he was able to trounce me at piquet, he seems perfectly competent to undertake some of the less strenuous responsibilities of managing the house," she said tartly. "I mean, really, of course, it needs a mistress. But it seems rather too much to hope Ned will be marrying any time soon. By the by, on that topic, Miss Green and I were wondering if you needed rescuing."

"*What?*" He was so very glad that the light was bad, and to his advantage, as he was taller and had control over the height of the candelabrum. There was no way she would be able to discern the wild blush on his face.

"We thought it well within Ned's bad manners to make you promise not to marry and set up a household of your own if you wanted to keep this position. If he did, then I'll speak to him on your behalf. I don't approve of it."

John was incapable of doing anything but gasping with horrified laughter. He had to set the candelabrum down on the table trapping him to the left. He leaned against the wall and put his hands over his face. "Ha ha ha ha!"

"You know him well enough to acknowledge it isn't out of the *question*," said Miss Fairwell, sounding cross.

"Th-th-thank you for your concern, Miss Fairwell." He couldn't stop laughing. It was much better to laugh than it was to think about her skirt against his legs and the fact that they were in the almost-dark without a chaperon. It had not even occurred to her that she *should* have a chaperon. Because as far as she was concerned he was her brother's employee and except for that *last* bit, they had been discussing estate business in a mostly-professional capacity.

"That's rather personal," he managed to get out at last, "but rest assured I don't need rescuing from your brother. He isn't Bluebeard."

"I would have considered myself remiss if I hadn't checked."

He would have been remiss if he hadn't tried to extricate himself from this situation. Yet his mind provided no immediate method for it.

"Will you show me the windows in need of panes?" Miss Fairwell said.

And that turned into a complete tour of the upper storey. At Gatewood House, the servants' quarters were in the basement, so the upstairs would have served as the family and guest quarters. Only the three chambers on the east side were habitable.

"Hm, it's good there wasn't one more of us," said Miss Fairwell, noting the fact. "We would've had to share a bed."

Naturally, John knew, she meant "we" as "Miss Green and Miss Fairwell," though he stared at the wall for a second trying unsuccessfully to rid his mind of other possibilities.

He didn't know if it was better or worse that, as far as he could tell, she wasn't mentioning bed-sharing with the slightest intent of flirtation. He had observed, in all of the Fairwells he so far numbered among his acquaintance, that they seemed to have dense streaks.

All he could be glad of was that this couldn't last too much longer, as the bell for dinner would sound in—it couldn't be more than an hour.

He showed her the windows in two of the rooms on the west side, which had broken in a storm earlier in the year and had been boarded up rather than fixed.

"Did Ned actually *forbid* you from having them fixed?"

John wasn't entirely willing to answer. He affected not to hear.

"Mr Stanger!"

"Pardon?"

"Did my brother *tell* you to *not* fix the windows?"

"Ah...he didn't want to be bothered by the workmen."

Miss Fairwell pressed her lips together. "You know what I think of that, Mr Stanger?"

"Possibly something not terribly flattering to my friend or myself, Miss Fairwell."

She lost her stern expression. "Very well, Mr Stanger, fair enough." She took a step toward him. She was near enough the window that he could see how intently she was looking at him. "After everything you've done for my brother, it seems uncharitable for me to think anything but the most flattering things about you."

Perhaps she was flirting with him. Was she? She seemed quite serious.

He had the urge to ward her off with a wave of the candelabrum. Instead, he made himself smile. "I was a draper's son serving as Ensign in His Majesty's Army. I assure you, I'm accustomed to accepting criticism."

The criticisms given by Miss Fairwell—being deserved, and

forgiving, and coming with the promise of assistance as it did—caused but a little dent in his pride. Compared to the unending petty cruelty of his fellow officers—which had felt like being buried six feet deep in Portuguese mud, every day anew, with nothing but his hands to dig himself out....compared to that...a genuine, well-deserved scolding was practically a ray of sunshine.

"How *did* you become friends with my brother?" she asked, just curious. "You are rather *different* from each other."

He didn't know what to say. He almost answered, simply: "I'm not going to tell you." He almost *did* tell her, but she would either think badly of him, or she would sympathize, and he didn't want either of those things.

"The same way any men become friends; through shared adversity. Let me show you the best room on this floor, Miss Fairwell." He gestured to the door.

She followed him out. "My, you do have a way with changing the topic."

"It isn't a pleasant topic."

Well, *that* was true. She could imagine it was Boney's doing if she wanted.

The room at the back of the house had one large circular window in the centre of the south wall, like a ship's porthole but larger by an order of magnitude. The panes had been designed in a pattern known as "rose," but with its long petals it seemed more like a grand daisy.

Miss Fairwell went up to it at once and peered out.

"How charming! What was this room used for?"

"A chapel, perhaps, given the window? Though, given the Eckerleys, probably—"

"—a picture gallery...."

He chuckled. "Right."

She looked around at the frame. "It's deep enough to sit in but I need a few more inches. Will you help me up?"

He could think of no rational reason to say no; it wasn't high enough to be dangerous. He put the unnecessary candelabrum down out of the way. Her arm went around his neck. His hands found her waist and without any fuss he lifted her a few inches to her perch.

And it would have been perfectly inconsequential as long as she'd taken her arm away. But she didn't. Her arm stayed crooked around his neck. She was now about the same height as he was.

She met his eyes with a smile. Her skirts were pressed all around his legs, or perhaps it was the other way around. Her bow was getting crushed against his chest.

The happy smile and the hand gently resting on the back of his neck had definitely answered the question of whether the chemistry was mutual, but he had no idea whether she was just innocently enjoying the discovery or if she had been planning to seduce him for a while. It was possible he'd been the dense one.

She smelled spectacularly good—like roses. Roses weren't in bloom yet. That was because it was an expensive French scent. Ah. She adjusted her hand behind his neck and she was obviously going to lean forward and kiss him and that could comprehensively ruin both their lives.

He hastily took his hands off her waist and stepped back. She steadied herself against the window frame, staring at him with giant startled eyes. Well, he didn't think it had been an organized attempt at seduction, he'd give her that.

He cleared his throat. "Pardon me, I—I have an appointment." Yes! That could be true!

She tried to smile, but her eyes were wavering somewhere around his shoulders and his chin. She swallowed. "Who are you meeting? It'll be dinner soon, you'll miss it."

Getting the words out was actually more difficult than being shot at by Frenchmen.

"A girl."

He had made himself keep looking at her as he said it and he saw every bit of the wince, which went from the top of her curls down to her slippered toes. She closed her eyes for a second.

But perhaps it was good, like having a tooth out. No going back.

After the wince had passed she looked him in the eye and smiled at him, not perfectly, but close enough.

"A girl from the village?"

"Where else?"

"Well. I wish you happy!"

"Thank you. Do you need a hand down?"

"No, I'm quite all right."

Downstairs, John stuck his head into the library. "Going out!"

He bit his tongue until he was all the way down the drive. All the way past the church. And striding at full speed down a wooded lane before he let himself swear and feel sorry for himself.

Had he scared her off permanently? By God, he hoped so. He had tried to overreach himself with the Army commission and he'd sworn never to do it again.

A gentlewoman like Kitty Fairwell wasn't going to marry her brother's semi-competent estate steward; and he certainly wasn't going to seduce his best friend's little sister, who very possibly had never been kissed.

Or perhaps she'd wrapped her legs around men in every cloak-room in London. From his point of view it *didn't matter*. (He swore a lot more. This walk was very uncomfortable and that mental image wasn't helping.) Plenty of women in the world, even (especially!) women who didn't wear silk and smell of attar of roses.

He reached a particularly well-kept cottage with a trickle of smoke rising out of the chimney. He took a breath and knocked on the door.

No one answered. He stared at the door. Well, this was what he got for showing up right before dinner time. He knocked again rather more loudly.

Molly Weaver opened the door wearing an apron. She was a

good-looking woman with just a few years on him, with brown eyes and plump cheeks; she'd been through two husbands already.

Understandably, she looked surprised to see him.

Unexpectedly, she edged outside the door and closed it behind her, rather than inviting him in.

He reached to take off his hat and then discovered he'd forgotten to put it on.

"You have company," he said. "Sorry, I won't disturb you."

He was pretty certain Molly had at least one other lover, but she was discreet and warm and talented at making sure they both enjoyed themselves in ways that wouldn't end up with a baby.

She gave him a look that boded ill, though she had the grace to look sorry about it.

"Well, John, d'you want the bad news now or later?"

He sighed. "Go on, Mol."

"I'm expecting."

John stared at her for a minute. She had a giant grin so he supposed it wasn't his place to say any damn thing.

"Felicitations."

"That's a hell of a fancy word," she said reasonably. She knew what he meant.

"Yes. Who's the father?"

"The blacksmith." She gave him a sudden dark look. "*No duels.*"

"Never fear," said John, swallowing all ironic comment on the impossibility of him challenging the blacksmith to a duel. "You haven't posted banns?" He hadn't heard them called in church. And he hadn't been *that* distracted.

"Oh, we will, only I've made him promise me he'll give me a new roof first."

"*I* would have given you a new roof, Mol," John said irritably.

"Yes, but because it was your business, not because you were in love with me," she said, gently and sensibly.

He took a deep breath and said, "Fair enough. Best of luck to all three of you, eh?"

She looked at him with soft eyes. "A kiss good-bye?"

He obliged, for old time's sake. On mutual unspoken agreement it turned into an embrace.

She patted him on the rear. "Too bad!" She stepped back and sized him up. She had the expression of taking pity on him. "You know Sadie Jones? She's just given up on a prospect. I believe she fancies you. I don't think you'd go wrong if you knocked on her door."

"I'll think about it," he said, to save arguing.

He put on an imaginary hat. She laughed. They said good-bye again and he started off.

"Hey! D'you need a lantern?" she called after him.

He judged the sun in the sky and kept walking. "I'll make it if I hurry."

Just as well, he thought. Just as well. He did like Molly Weaver but if he'd got her in bed, he wouldn't have been thinking of her. And that didn't quite meet his own standard of behaviour—which was perhaps a bit better than most gentlemen's.

CHAPTER NINE

WHEN JOHN STANGER LEFT her sitting on the window-sill without a backward glance, Kitty sat immobile for a long moment.

She had almost kissed him.

Only belatedly did she feel overpowering horror at the realization of how cruel it would have been—and relief that he'd stopped it.

Ned probably wouldn't have fired him for just a kiss, but there would have been *words*, and she could imagine Mr Stanger doing a typically mannish thing like resigning on principal for his own bad behaviour. It would have ruined a friendship and lost Mr Stanger his employment and it would have been *entirely* her fault.

Thank heavens he'd put an end to it.

If only he'd waited about sixty seconds longer....

No! she was not going to think like that. It had *almost* happened, but it hadn't because Mr Stanger was a wise and quick-witted man, and he had gone off to kiss his paramour— Kitty was not sure if she actually existed or if she'd just been an excuse. Regardless, she was going to *believe very firmly* in her existence. The existence of a paramour was *wonderful* because the idea of kissing a man belonging to another woman was genuinely dreadful. That would stop her even if concerns like ruined friendships and lost employment *weren't* enough.

Ruined friendships, lost employment, and…she had a queer and uncomfortable thought. If they'd been caught, it wouldn't affect just *him*. She didn't think her family would disinherit her like the Greens had turned their backs on Louisa's father. Even so, she knew the stories people whispered in sitting-rooms, of bad choices made and every member of a family's prospects sullied. She winced all over. So thank *God* Mr Stanger had….

She knew she was forgetting something…but she'd forgotten what. She was running a fever. Actually, she was perfectly well aware that the overheated trembly sensation she was feeling was one common to barnyard animals. This was why people married, so they could take care of it properly. Perhaps when she went back to London she would meet an *appropriate* man who…

…oh, she….

Oh what a funny thought.

Engaged, she told herself. Engaged. Engaged. Yes, you. Percy's lips were sort of…limp. Like cold eels. But he did make you feel warm and…happy! Yes. Percy had been so adoring.

Kitty slid off the window, straightened her dress with dignity, and blew out the candelabrum which was sputtering down.

"Louisa?"

"Come in."

"How are you feeling?"

Louisa was lying on her stomach; she turned her face so she was looking in Kitty's direction. "Do you really want to know? I'm dreading tomorrow." She pulled herself up in several jerky motions, ending up sitting with her feet tucked up and her arms wrapped around herself. She dragged a blanket around herself and looked like an odd tangled tent with the head of a beautiful girl.

Kitty sat on the bed next to her. "Miss Horne doesn't treat you badly, does she?"

Louisa was silent. "She doesn't love me. She doesn't beat me. She was strict about learning what I needed to know to come out. Until recently I would have said I was grateful."

"If you could choose to do anything, what would you do?"

Louisa looked down at the quilt. Her fingers plucked a spare thread. "I'd go back to Bastable," she said in a low, cold voice.

"No!" Kitty cried. "Louisa, he beat you!"

"And if I could, I'd beat him in punishment. But that was after months of the most—the most—" she fell silent. "I don't imagine all fallen women enjoy it, but I did. I dream about him night and day. Don't mistake me, Kitty, I no longer want to be his wife. But his mistress to be held, and kissed, and whispered to, and stroked, and rutted with in every way the most experienced whore could possibly imagine—if I could go back to the way it was a month ago, as guilty as it was, I would sell my soul for it."

"*Louisa!*"

"Well, I would. I would." Her eyes gleamed with a terrible light that made Kitty inch away. "Passion was the only thing I've ever been good at."

"You have a beautiful voice," Kitty stammered.

"I have a beautiful voice. So do lots of girls. I should have been a courtesan." She shook her head sharply. "Except I haven't any charm. That was him. And it *was* him—is him—I want, not just anyone; it wouldn't be like that with anyone else. Him or nobody."

"He doesn't—he didn't—"

"Love me? Care about me?" She shrugged. "He would have married me; it was me who stopped it. For a man, does the thing women call 'love' really matter? Isn't soul-eating enrapturing lust enough?"

To this Kitty was able to squarely answer, "No, it's not enough. What would happen when you had children?"

"Considering what we did at every opportunity," Louisa said, "it seems rather unlikely that I can, if I haven't already. He said barrenness made me the perfect mistress."

She sounded proud rather than bitter, so Kitty painfully left it alone.

"Perhaps there will again be someone else you feel that way about," she said, "who has a better character."

"I won't be looking for him. I want free of this. I've been ruled by it since the moment I met him and I'm still under its control."

"You don't have to ever meet him again."

"Thank God."

Kitty looked at her carefully. "You won't be able to go back to London."

Louisa laughed harshly. "For so many reasons, no."

"You said that between you and Miss Horne you can manage. Is that true?"

"Yes. We can take a cottage in the country."

"You must know if you *ever* need help—"

"If you could pull this worm out of my heart—but—" Louisa's shoulders shrugged up and down under the blanket. "You are the best person I know, Kitty. You shame me."

"No, don't say that! I just want to know you're safe. Isn't that what anyone would want for their friends?"

Louisa pressed her lips together and angled her chin as if considering a thought. Finally she just said, "Yes, I suppose so. Kitty, may I ask for something?"

For the first time her voice trembled.

"Of course—ask."

"A little time. That's all I ask. A few more days before I have to leave this bed forever. It's like my nest, mine alone, and it reminds me that I—" she stuck her hand out from underneath the blanket and looked at it as if it belonged to someone else. "That I exist as myself. I know that sounds absurd. I can't explain it."

"Of course I can see that you have a few more days. I don't mind staying, and you're my guest. When Miss Horne comes, she can take in the room Will was in. Is that all right?"

"Yes. Yes, thank you."

Louisa leaned over and stuck an arm out of her tent to hug Kitty with ridiculous awkward coltishness.

The dinner bell rang.

"Oh, dear," said Kitty. "Either Jane is miffed at me, or I'm about to be miffed at Jane."

She found Jane reading *Pride and Prejudice* sprawled across Kitty's own bed. Jane blinked at her upside down.

"What *are* you wearing, Miss?"

"And what *are* you doing, Jane?"

Getting out of the dress took a long time and Kitty was already upset. She couldn't face dinner with Ned in this state.

Eventually, she ended up sending Jane down to filch some rolls and convey her regrets. Jane had a touch for dramatic mimicry; Ned wouldn't dare argue.

Point the *First*. She had a *tendre* for John Stanger, which was approximately equal parts lust and humorous adoration for the way his smile made his un-brows go up and down.

Point the *Second*. John Stanger clearly reciprocated, but he had a sweetheart and a job to keep.

Point the *Third*. She was in love with Percy Wolcott, which was a quieter and more thought-out matter than a *tendre*. Percy danced well; was always attentive to her needs; didn't gamble excessively; liked children; drove a carriage with a good mix of style and caution. He was also well-off enough that she could be certain he wasn't trying to marry her for her money. His sisters were completely tolerable companions, which was *important*. She liked his shoulders and his big hands. He had been endearingly awkward as he confessed how *happy* he was to find her, because he just wanted to settle down in the country already and it was *so* hard these days to find a girl who wasn't a schemer *and* understood horses.

Point the *Fourth*. It was *quite good* that Percy existed, because otherwise she might have had to wonder how it would hurt her family if she were tempted into a *mésalliance*. Will was going to want to marry some respectable girl—knowing him, probably a vicar's daughter—and the idea that he might miss his chance at love because of Kitty's actions was simply too painful to bear. She couldn't do that to him. And Susannah would want to remarry after Matthew died; and Robert and Henry *ought* to; and Susannah had three daughters not yet out.

Point the *Fifth*. She was going to marry Percy Wolcott. This was a good decision, as it was made with brain and heart, not loins. They were a good match.

Point the *Sixth*. Perhaps she could get Louisa to explain how kisses *ought* to feel so she could convey this to Percy. She believed that he could learn.

Point the *Seventh*. She was a *grown* and *civilized* woman and she could certainly maintain a circumspect distance from her brother's estate steward for however many few days she remained at Gatewood House. She had especial confidence in this, as said steward seemed to be of the same mind.

Said steward was at breakfast the next morning eating hurriedly as if he were running late for something.

He did not look...perfectly well-rested.

Kitty was unsure whether to be flattered, if it had been due to her, or jealous if it had been due to someone else. Drat. Apparently she *did* need it absolutely confirmed that his sweetheart was real and not imaginary, because in this state of unknowingness she still desperately wanted to request a lesson in kissing.

"Good morning, Ned. Good morning, Mr Stanger."

"Good morning, Miss Fairwell," said Mr Stanger, looking up from his toast exactly long enough to be polite.

Ned stared at her with his good eye, which even Kitty found mildly unnerving whilst eating kippers.

She had a spike of cold fear that he had *somehow* found out about the *almost-kiss*. But that was quite irrational. It was a creaky house, and even had a servant, unnoticed, passed by the door to the rose-window room at just the wrong moment, she suspected that all the servants liked Mr Stanger better than Ned.

He would not have escaped without a private warning from Howard or Mrs Dowell—but she doubted they would have run straight to Ned to rat him out.

Indeed, her fear was quite heedless. Ned had a different bone to pick.

"Will has gone off all mithered about something. He told me that Miss Green's—companion will be arriving soon. Companion? Relation?"

"An aunt. She raised her after Louisa was orphaned."

She didn't expect Ned to have sympathy on account of orphanry, but it couldn't hurt.

"Good. As soon as they're gone, I'll see you back to Mrs Whalen. I'm still trying to sort out how. Next time you come visit, by God, please bring an appropriate traveling companion. *Not* that terrifying maid, who seems like she'd slit my throat as soon as my back is turned."

"Isn't that what one looks for in a lady's companion?" Kitty said blandly. "If your concern is my safety, how is a maid who can also slit throats not *ideal?*"

Mr Stanger was choking on his tea. Ned grabbed for his cane and braced himself to get up. Mr Stanger shook his head and waved his hand, smiling in a sickly fashion as if to signal: No, perfectly all right, not requiring a thump on the back!

Ned sank back down, watching to make sure his friend was still breathing.

"I wish I could send John to escort you."

"Perhaps one of the footmen," suggested Kitty mildly. She considered mentioning the business of hiring two maids, as well as glaziers, carpenters for the roof, and a substantial order for the drapers, but decided now was not the moment.

Mr Stanger gulped the last of his tea, gave one last muffled cough, and rose. "I'll be in the Italian room," he remarked to the room at large.

There was nothing exceptionally Italian about any of the rooms Kitty had seen, so she had to think it was the room she *hadn't* seen, which was to say, the locked room adjoining the library.

She gave him a friendly nod as he took his leave. She believed

Mr Stanger was correct in thinking that there was going to be a raging argument in a moment.

Whilst she *would* have been grateful to have a disinterested party present when faced with Ned's temper, she also understood why Mr Stanger was considering discretion the better part of valour. After all, it wasn't as if he could get between them.

She tried not to feel abandoned. She scolded herself at the very thought!

She drew in a breath. *The Fearless Fairwells aren't just the* men.

"I have to warn you, Ned, I made a promise to Miss Green. She needs a few more days before Miss Horne whisks her off goodness knows where. I'm staying here with her."

Ned took that as well as she'd expected.

"No you are most certainly *not!*" he roared. "She is off with Miss Horne if I have to pay for a post-chaise myself."

"My, you have a loud voice," said Kitty with detachment. Really, it knocked you over like a gale. She imagined Wellington must have found him exceptionally useful.

"*You* can go to Mrs Whalen, or back to Grandbourne as you like, but *yesterday* wouldn't be too soon for you to end your acquaintance with Miss Green."

"Don't tell me you're getting prim at your age."

Her hands were shaking under the table; she couldn't specifically remember being yelled at before. She remembered Ned and Julia and occasionally Susannah and even more rarely Robert having some loud wrangles throughout the years, but *she* was the baby of the family and had never received anything more than a scolding. "What is the harm? She's been here four days already; another three hurts nothing."

Ned lowered his voice somewhat, but she wasn't sure if his sarcastic tone was more tolerable.

"*You're* the one who spent every minute of her life plotting her escape from Grandbourne into that hypocritical cesspool known as the *ton*. The devil knows why. But you can't decide to play their games by rules you've made up. Every minute you spend with that Green girl is spreading a stain over your reputation."

"Any *decent* gentlemen *I'd* be interested in marrying would understand why I had to get Louisa away from Harry Bastable."

She thought that was a point to her.

"It's not the gentlemen you should be worried about," he hissed, "it's their *mamas*. They will drop you like a hot iron. She seduced the perfectly respectable scion of a good family and when he tried to do the right thing she wouldn't have him. *He'll* be patted on the head. *She's* no better than a common harlot."

"He seduced *her!*" Then she took a breath, because she knew perfectly well it didn't matter. "Let me be *very* clear with you, Ned Fairwell. I do not fool myself that Louisa is blameless, but Harry Bastable is not a man any woman should marry. Wife-beating may be legal in this country but will you honestly sit there and swear to me that if one of your tenant's wives turned up black and blue that you would sit back and do nothing? I actually imagine you would quite enjoy terrifying the breath out of his lungs."

He blinked at her, fish-like. "You're not stupid enough to think that's the same. It's a *pity* she doesn't have a father or brothers who can shoot the little lick-twat in Hyde Park at dawn. That she doesn't, doesn't make it *your* problem. If you decide you don't care what the *ton* thinks it's all the same to me, but you're my sister and *I* care what sort of company you keep. Get rid of her. Get rid of her, confess you made a charity case of her because you read that ninny Hannah More one too many times, disavow you were ever *friends*. Perhaps you'll get away with it. But you *will* get rid of her."

"You are quite right," Kitty said.

He looked at her with deep suspicion.

"About what society might say. But we *are* friends," she shouted. "If I gave up my friends as soon as they needed help, just for the sake of my own convenience, I would be ashamed to look at myself in the mirror. I would be ashamed to share my mother's name!"

Ned pointed a finger at her. "I knew your mother. She had better taste in friends!"

Kitty gasped. "Even *you* have a friend, so you're hardly in a position to judge other people for their tastes!"

"Don't you *dare!*"

"Fancy *that*—you think I've insulted Mr Stanger and you turn colours. Well, get it through your thick head, the feeling of loyalty is not strictly shared by the male sex! My friend needs me, and she has asked for something quite within my ability to provide. Which is nothing more than a few day's time. Her entire future is in ruins—"

"Through her own actions!"

"Shouldn't you *of all people* understand why someone might need time to recover from tragedy just as if from illness? You're perfectly capable of leading an ordinary life—so many men would consider themselves lucky to have escaped with so little injury as you; you even kept your leg! And yet here you are, two years later and still skulking around in a house with broken windows just because it suits you not to *try!* 'Fearless' Fairwell my arse!"

He banged his fist on the table and all the china jumped. Kitty ducked instinctively, her heart pounding in her chest.

"GET OUT," said Ned.

Chapter Ten

"My, you have a loud voice," said Miss Fairwell as John walked away. She sounded stunned.

John could hear every word of Ned's response.

John was *completely* opposed to eavesdropping. Both in general, and especially if Ned wanted to scold his sister. It was not any of his business.

So he should have pushed the door to the Italian room closed behind him. All the way closed.

He stood inside with his hand on it, willing himself to push it the final three inches. He could hear the first strains of raised voices from the saloon, right around the corner from his door. Both politeness and common sense clearly demanded he stay well away from this. Also, he had work to do.

A small motion was all that was necessary.

On the other hand…he had born the brunt of some of Ned's rages himself. And whilst Ned wasn't a physically violent man, the force of his roar could feel about the same. Miss Fairwell was a small woman and from what Ned had said about her childhood and generally obliging character, John couldn't imagine she got scolded much in her life. He couldn't bring himself to leave her completely without support—if it turned out she needed it.

Or perhaps it was Ned who would need rescuing. He had soft spots, and he wasn't good at recovering if jabbed in one.

He couldn't catch every word, but Ned's voice rose again.

"…plotting her escape from Grandbourne into that hypocritical cesspool known as the *ton*. The devil knows why…."

John took his hand off the door without closing it. "I'm going to regret this," he said to himself, too softly for anyone to hear.

*

A few minutes later he had given up the idea of going to his desk. He stood leaning against the wall by the cracked door with his arms crossed. There had been a few seconds in which he almost shoved it closed, on the grounds that if eavesdropping were bad, eavesdropping on a conversation in which you were mentioned was courting a desperately lonely life. But Kitty's point was fair.

Not that it was his place to judge, but it was clear to him that they were both right. Kitty *would* be judged for her loyalty to Miss Green, and from the point of view of logic she ought to disavow her as quickly as possible.

And it made his heart swell up with happiness that she would not do it. How could he be proud of her? She wasn't his to be proud of. It would have been far better if he were disgusted with her. Instead her willingness to stick up for her friend fanned his regard which was—already too warm. All right. Overheated. She was a brave, passionate young lady and *of course* he fancied her; every young buck in London probably did too. Fancying her was harmless as long as he kept it to himself.

"*—perfectly capable of—so many men—lucky to have escaped—kept your leg!*" Her voice reached a pitch. "*And yet here you are, two years later and still skulking around in a house with broken windows just because it suits you not to try! 'Fearless' Fairwell my arse!*"

John sighed. Well, that was a good way to cool his ardor. Some of the heat transmuted to a small licking flame of anger, on Ned's behalf.

There was a crash, but no cry.

"*GET OUT!*"

He heard her shoes on the floor of the staircase hall, staccato and angry. He should have closed his door. Too late; it was better to leave it—

No. Sharply, he pulled the door open.

He wasn't an impetuous man. It just seemed like this was part of what he promised himself he'd do—taking care of Ned.

Miss Fairwell was passing through the staircase hall and she spun, startled, seeing him suddenly appear in the side of her vision. She looked flushed and wild and trembly, like a small angry beast. He could dishevel her like that if he got her into bed and she'd look a lot happier about it. No, he was not doing that. (Even a little? Even a little?)

He motioned her toward him with a sharp jerk of his hand and stepped back. Her eyes narrowed. She threw her head back. She spun on her heel and stalked toward the front of the house. He stayed where he was, deciding.

He heard the front door open and close with a bang. Without being entirely clear when he'd decided to follow, he went after her.

She hadn't gone very far. As soon as he set foot outside, he spotted her sitting on one of the sets of steps leading down from the front door.

"Listen, Miss Fairwell," he said sharply down to the curly back of her head. "Let's talk." He amended quickly, "about your brother." He supposed there were other ways she could have taken it and he wanted to stave them off.

She straightened her back but didn't look round at him. "Were you listening?" she said in a clear voice.

"Of course I was listening; that's my damn room right there and I wanted to be sure you weren't going to break out in fisticuffs."

He went down the steps to just below her, and leaned against the wall of the house, so he could look at her without being too close. She stared at him with defiance in her eyes, although he also saw that she had wiped off her face quickly.

"Whatever argument you have with your brother is none of my interest," he said, unmoved by the remaining trace of a tear on her chin. "But just because you're his sister doesn't mean you get to be cruel to him."

"I don't want to be cruel to him. But I think *you* cosset him. I think you let him stay in his library and you don't push him to keep up on even his most undemanding responsibilities. Doesn't it occur to you that through being kind, you're holding him back? That the thing a friend might truly do would be to give him a good shove?"

"This *is* pushing him," said John in exasperation. "How many times have you seen him since he was wounded?"

"Twice."

"In London both times."

"I imagine you know the details just as well as I."

John said very evenly, "I know it was in London because he weeps like a baby after an hour in a carriage; he wanted to see you all at Grandbourne but he might not be able to ever travel that far again. If you can manage to live your life without watching a man sob from pain for hours on end, I recommend it."

She looked stricken but didn't do anything missish like bursting into tears. "Any of us would have been happy to come here. He didn't have to travel to see us!"

"Don't be a fool. He didn't want any of you here. Because you'd stay for longer than invited, and you'd prod, and you'd notice that he slept most of the day and perhaps that he woke up screaming at night." He kept standing there, looking at her inexorably. "He lay on the battlefield five hours before I found him, and he was awake for every damn second of it, waiting to die and hoping he would just so the pain would stop. So it's not just pain, it's memory."

Ned had said: "Every time another looting party of frogs went through my pockets I asked them to kill me. '*Désolé, monsieur.*' So damned polite. 'Out of bullets. *Désolé.* Don't worry, your people will be by soon.'" But John wasn't about to repeat that.

Miss Fairwell was looking at his shoes. "Do you have bad dreams, Mr Stanger?" she asked in a low voice.

"When I think back to what I saw, makes my heart hurt. But

not all men are the same. Like carriages with different wheels and springs, we feel as God made us. I have different griefs."

After so many years his dreams of Maria and Cora were few and vague. Perhaps that was the worst thing about them.

John said flatly, "They should have just cut his leg off on the field, but the surgeon felt he was having a clever day. For a long time, he talked about having it off to stop the pain."

Miss Fairwell pressed her hand over her mouth.

"It might be the right thing to do. I've always tried to talk him out of it. I don't want to lose him from infection. I was wounded and I almost died of it, though it was barely a scratch. So I'm afraid.

"Did any of your brothers tell you he was addicted to laudanum for a while? That was my job for most of the first year. Meting it out drop by drop and trying to guess when I could believe him, when he said the pain was unbearable that day. If he got too much he'd try to walk on the leg, and it would start to seep again. Those were pretty bad days, Miss Fairwell."

"No wonder you think me cruel."

"No, I think perhaps you're right," he said. "Perhaps. Not definitely. You see an ill-tempered, wounded man who has the use of his brain and his hands and his tongue, so why doesn't he do better with them? Isn't that it? And I've seen him when he was barely able to speak. This is so much better than he was I consider it a triumph. And that's where the problem is. Of course I wonder exactly the thing you do. He'd probably stay in his library the rest of his days if I let him. But it's like with the laudanum. How much is healing, and how much is just hiding? We don't have any way of knowing, do we?"

Miss Fairwell was silent, dragging a finger back and forth across the line of a step. "I apologize, Mr Stanger."

"I don't need it." He thought better. "Thank you."

She glanced up at him. "I suppose I'd better apologize to Ned, too. I'm not wrong about Louisa. But I don't want to be cruel." She looked over her shoulder in the approximate direction of the library and sighed. "Perhaps...I should wait until he calms down. No, no, if I put it off I won't do it."

He took a deep breath and offered her a hand up. "Would you like me to warn him you're coming in, so the roar won't start on the instant?"

She accepted the hand, giving him a quick smile. "Oh, I would very much appreciate that. Thank you."

"If it helps any, he utterly adores you."

A more lingering smile this time. "I know."

After a few words to Ned, he bowed Miss Fairwell into the library. He couldn't do Miss Fairwell's work for her, but he'd given her what little help he could.

This time he closed the door *all* the way.

Having eavesdropped already once, he didn't want to work in the Italian room, with its connecting door to the library: it was clear he couldn't pass by temptation. At least not that kind of temptation. He quickly collected his account books and repaired to the saloon, where the light was good most of the day.

After ten minutes he was barely through his first column of figures and was already missing 6*d*. (Will Fairwell was right, he was a scrupulous bookkeeper—but it usually took several draughts.) The distant sound of the butler greeting someone at the front door startled him. A visitor was unusual enough that he lowered his pen quite amazed.

He wondered if he should take his things back to the Italian room—in case they really *did* have guests, and it wasn't merely some traveler under the misapprehension that the Eckerleys and their art collection were still in residence.

Ah, but of course, it would have to be Miss Horne! He hastily wiped his pen, returned the cap to the ink and picked up his books. He'd done enough getting his nose in the business of his betters for the day.

As he walked back to his room, by necessity toward the front of the house, he could faintly hear Howard, and a piercing female voice, and an excited-sounding tenor. The presence of the histrionic tenor gave him pause. Only a rich man would dare try to do so much with so little. Yet he'd understood that Miss Green didn't have any male relations. So who....

He had a dreadful feeling about this.

He dropped his account books on his desk and went (once again) to see if Ned needed rescuing.

John stood back and surveyed the crowd, taking it all in.

The front hall was occupied by Ned, Miss Fairwell, Howard the butler, Adam the younger footman, Ned's valet the bullfrog-faced John Quire—and four more: an older female servant, a well-dressed male one; the bony, pinch-faced lady who was producing that unpleasant voice that echoed off the ceiling of the hall; and the tenor.

John had a sneaking suspicion who the tenor was. From the way Miss Fairwell looked keen to punch him, he considered the suspicion confirmed. Ned's free hand was resting heavily on her shoulder, and John didn't think it was for balance.

Harry Bastable was slightly plump and boyish-looking, but had an active carriage and a cool way of looking around himself with short smooth deliberate glances as if he wanted to know where everyone was at all times. John wondered if he boxed—but his nose was still good. His clothes were of first-rate cloth though they were cut with generous room to move, rather than wrapping his shoulders and thighs up like sausages. A sporting gentleman, then, not a dandy.

Even if John hadn't known he'd hurt Miss Green, he probably would have wanted to punch him on general principles. He was exactly the sort of man who bought an officer's commission and was then surprised that there was actual *work* involved.

John listened for a second and at once gathered the gist of the argument between Miss Fairwell and the pinch-faced lady, who was surely Miss Horne. Was he really *surprised* at this turn of events? He supposed, in retrospect, he shouldn't be.

"She has *no other option*," insisted Miss Horne shrilly to Miss Fairwell. "Cease shrieking at me at once! You have been an unforgivable influence on Louisa but that comes to an end *now*. Will someone tell her to fetch her things." This was vaguely directed in Howard's direction.

"I *BEG YOUR PARDON*," said Ned, his face dark. "That is MY SISTER you are speaking to."

Miss Horne was not immune to gale-force voice booming toward her. She froze.

Out of interest, John was watching Harry Bastable. He too froze, though for only a breath. He looked impressed. He slowly sized up how heavily Ned was leaning on his cane.

John slid around the outside of the fracas and arrived on Ned's right. Bad leg, good eye. Pugnacious John Quire and Adam the tall whip of a footman were on Ned's left; that was good….

"MISS HORNE," said Ned implacably. "It is illegal in this country to force a woman to marry. Miss Green does not want to marry Mr Bastable."

"Let me just *see* her," said Bastable, sounding reasonable, polite, even a little pleading. "I know she's upset with me, but I'll make it up to her. I can't live without her—I really can't!"

"*You*, sir, are not welcome in this house and I expect you to remove yourself at once. As for *you*, Miss Horne, I will speak with you in private." Ned's tone of voice conveyed that he would rather have licked horse dung off his boots, but one had to do what one must.

"Miss Green is my fiancée!" said Bastable. "Fairwell, there's no point in you meddling in my affairs. Let me collect her and we won't trouble you a moment more."

"I'll go with him," said Louisa Green, soft but clear.

All heads turned.

She was as pale as a ghost dressed in pink muslin. Even across the room John could see the hollows of her cheeks.

Jane Addams was behind her with a vicious glare for Bastable.

"Louisa!" cried Bastable with apparent genuine delight. "Sweetheart!" He started toward her.

Howard and Adam closed ranks in front of her, bless their souls.

"You stay where you are," Ned snarled at Bastable; "this is my house and you haven't been invited in."

Bastable had the sense to stop moving.

"Adam!" rapped out Ned to the footman. "And you,—" he gestured. "Terrifying maid!"

"Jane, sir," said Jane imperturbably.

"Keep Miss Green over there."

Neither of the young servants hesitated; Adam, towering above her, took one arm, and Jane, sturdy and unafraid to bull her way onward, took the other. Miss Green made a noise of protest but didn't fight. Kitty went to stand beside Howard. John stuck close to Ned.

With two flicks of his fingers Bastable undid buttons of his coat and produced a sheet of paper. He held it up. "Louisa! I have our marriage license. We can be wed tomorrow morning."

"Let me see that," said Ned, roaring and hobbling forward at the same time. He reached out his hand. With a shrug Bastable let him take it.

Ned glanced at it. Then, very quickly, with one hand and two fingers, he ripped it in two.

"You villain," said the astonished Bastable.

Ned ripped and ripped again, fiendishly, wobbling. He let the shreds snow down onto the floor and hastily rebalanced himself.

Bastable's face suffused with anger.

He reached inside his coat once more and produced a pistol.

The room at once became extremely loud and full of motion.

John stepped forward, trying to track what was going on.

Miss Horne and her maid rapidly shrank away from Bastable as if he were contagious.

Ned bellowed, "EVERYONE CLEAR OUT!"

As far as John could see, only Howard took it to heart. The butler grabbed young Adam's shoulder and hauled him into the staircase hall. Young Adam kept hold of Miss Green, and Jane kept hold of Miss Green, and as they all crossed the threshold she slammed the never-closed door shut after them. John hoped the butler was quick with the keys.

Bastable dived toward that door, almost smashing into Miss Fairwell who had planted herself in the way. He swiftly raised his pistol toward the ceiling, obviously not wishing to hurt her. As he tried to get around her she moved back into his path once again.

"KITTY, YOU FOOL, GET AWAY FROM HIM," roared Ned.

John ran forward desperately. "Kitty!"

With Bastable in the way, all he could see was her elbow and the quick motion of a foot as she had to step back. The two of them might have been dancing.

John heeled around Bastable and grabbed Kitty from the side. She yelled in surprise and fury as he hauled her bodily away from Bastable's path. She pulled away from him; they overbalanced and half fell. John shoved her away. He wasn't worried about Bastable reaching the door. By the time he'd manage to kick it down, the servants would have had ample time to drag Miss Green downstairs and barricade the entrance to the basement.

John couldn't see Bastable try the door behind him, but he heard an oath followed almost instantly by a pistol retort with a flat wrong sound after it.

His back suddenly hurt very much.

He let go of Kitty and put his hand on his back. It came away bloody.

He said the nastiest thing he could think of and sat down on the tiled floor. There was a sound in his ears like the sound inside of a seashell.

"Mr Stanger!" said Kitty Fairwell. He looked up. Inside of a black border blurring his vision, she looked terrified. "John!"

"No doctor, please," he said with difficulty, and then passed out.

CHAPTER ELEVEN

RIGHT IN FRONT OF HER, John Stanger half-fell, half-sat on the floor, saying some foul things with an air of detached surprise as he looked at his hand. Kitty saw fresh bright blood running down his fingers, unmistakable for anything else. She cried out.

He fell over the rest of the way. She threw herself down onto the tiles beside him, pulling him toward her to see his back. Her hand at once felt wet. Oh God! He was going to die in her arms and it was her fault. What had happened? Bastable shot him in the back? *Why?*

Some female voices were shrieking in fright—it was possible one of them was hers—and Ned was roaring for the servants to come back in and help. Kitty heard Bastable shouting, "It was an accident! A ricochet! I didn't—" The shout was ended with a giant crack and a cry of pain.

But even as that was going on, without quite considering, she was shoving up the sticky wet coat. It didn't move easily but after a second she pushed it out of the way and could see his handsome red waistcoat which was not supposed to be *that* colour red—almost black.

Rather surprisingly she found her hands being shoved out of the way by someone who had just knelt on his other side. She jerked her head up. Who the deuce—? It was Ned's bull-frog valet.

"*Space*, please, Miss Fairwell." He held up a hand. Metal glinted. He had a razor! Instinctively, she jerked backwards, but John's body was leaning across her lap and she couldn't pull away without letting him smash facedown onto the floor.

But the valet looked down at once. He professionally hooked one hand under the edge of John's waistcoat, set the edge of the razor to it and sliced it open. Then his linen shirt got the same treatment. Kitty steadied herself again. Her legs were starting to go numb under John's weight, but never mind.

"Are you a medical man?" she gasped.

A cane and shoes appeared in the corner of her vision. Then Ned knelt down with a disorganized crash and a muffled shout of agony. He bent over his friend, gently pulling up John's sagging head to feel for a pulse at his throat.

"As if," said John Quire in response to Kitty's question. He was pressing hard on the wound with one hand and prodding around it with the other. He had a thoughtful expression. "Nah, just a dab hand at duels from my last job. 'Course, that's *usually* in the front.

"Looks like it might be stuck in the muscle. Not too deep. That's good. Get me something to rinse off this blood so I can see, eh?"

The other servants had come back in at some point—Kitty wasn't sure when. Somebody brought brandy, and the valet used it liberally to wash away a dreadful quantity of blood. He squinted at the wound.

The bull-frog's eye fell on Kitty. "You've got little fingers. How's your stomach?"

Kitty stared at him with incomprehension.

"'Cause if you're going to puke I'd rather you shove off, but otherwise make yourself useful."

"Kitty," snapped Ned, "he wants you to see if you can get the bullet out."

"Oh-h!" exclaimed Kitty. Her stomach turned but she shot back: "Why didn't you say so?"

John Quire sat back, still keeping pressure on the wound with one giant palm. "I can feel it, but not get at it. It's close to the spine so it's best out. Give me your hand."

Kitty gritted her teeth. *Fearless Fairwells Fearless Fairwells* she repeated to herself. Shaking like a leaf, she held out her hand. The valet took her tiny fingers with his giant ones and guided them to a spot just above the entry wound and pressed them into the blood and flesh. Kitty couldn't help but whimper; then she was at once ashamed of herself. She swallowed, fighting with all her might to hold down her rising gorge.

"It's about there, but you'll need to go in and up. Right?"

"Yes, I see," said Kitty between gritted teeth. Then he was shifting his other hand so she could get access.

There was no help for it. She stuck her fingers into the wound, a dark roundish rent among a sheet of sticky red blood. Apparently she was going to whimper like a ninny as she did this, but she was going to do it regardless.

I have seen puppies and foals and calves being born, this is not *worse than that*— yes it was, it was definitely worse than that.

She wiggled her fingers around, trying to feel something hard.

"Feel it?"

"No!"

"Dig a bit," said the valet unhelpfully. "And if you feel fabric, that comes out too."

"Ned, stop breathing down my neck!" She shoved; there was a squishing sound; she gagged. "Oh! I do feel it!" It didn't feel bullet-shaped anymore; it had flattened out. Desperately hoping she could get it on the first try, she wedged the very tips of her fingers around it, clamped down and *pulled*.

And it was *out*, with a piece of cloth stuck to it, and she was happy for—about a second. Then she realized it was entirely possible John would still die. There was absolutely nothing to be happy about.

Howard and the second footman Thomas were crowding around, gently taking John's weight off her.

A hand took her gently but firmly by the shoulder. "Let's get you cleaned up, Miss," said Jane. Bloodthirsty girl, she sounded quite pleased with everything.

"I can't feel my feet," said Kitty, fuzzy-headed and able to focus on only one detail at a time. She stared down at herself; her hands were bloody and her dress was ruined. "Is Ned all right? He needs help up."

"Adam's got him. He's off with Mr Stanger."

Jane had good sense and Kitty had never been so glad of it. Doll-like, she allowed Jane to take her downstairs to the kitchen. The housekeeper, Mrs Dowell, had her stand in a tub—she supposed she was still dripping. The skirt of her dress was soaked through and clinging to her legs. After a little discussion Jane and Mrs Dowell cut off the whole dress and tossed it into the fire.

"Can I keep these stays?" Kitty mumbled, staring at her bare and blood-streaked toes against the copper bottom of the tub. They must have taken her slippers at some point. "I don't have any others here. And I like them."

Mrs Dowell bent to give her torso a look. "Yes, a bit of a scrub might set them right. Just smudges. Your chemise, I'm afraid—well, we could try boiling, but—"

Kitty had a dreadful image of wearing a shift with John's blood-stain on it, and she trembled. "Burn it."

So they divested her of her clothes and gave her a wash with warm water, despite which she shivered like a leaf. Once she was ensconced in someone's large green quilted robe Mrs Dowell sat her by the kitchen fire.

"Thank you, thank you," said Kitty, vaguely aware that she was crying. "Oh, I'm terribly sorry."

"Lud, Miss Fairwell, it's nothing to apologize for," said Mrs Dowell.

"As long as you stay put," said the less sympathetic cook, hurrying by with a pot, "or you'll get burned."

"Hush," said Mrs Dowell to the cook, and then to Kitty: "Jane said you were right brave. Mr Stanger's a fine young man and we're all grateful for what you did. When things quiet down upstairs Jane'll take you up and put you to bed, but for right now you just stay there and get warm."

Jane brought Kitty a rather large glass of brandy. "Courtesy of your brother."

"Ned sent me this?"

"Certainly," lied Jane with a glint in her eye.

Kitty sipped cautiously. "What's going on up there? Where's Louisa!" That was said with sudden startlement. Oh. She wasn't sure if she was angry with Louisa.

"Having it out with Miss Horne," said Jane darkly. Then, with a bit of pleasure, "It's good to see Miss Green has got some spice to her, pardonmemiss."

"And John—Mr Stanger," Kitty asked tremulously. "Is he s-s-s-still—"

Jane's eyebrows arched up neatly at "John" rather than "Mr Stanger." "Awake and would rather not be, I gather."

Kitty clutched the robe tightly around herself.

"And Bastable, is he—"

"Ooh, your brother gave him a great big wallop."

"Too bad it couldn't be a whipping," muttered Mrs Dowell.

"He's going to have a right interesting bruise," Jane went on. "Howard and Adam…saw him out." A nasty smile.

Kitty woke up in her own bed at some point when it was mostly dark outside her window. She lay confused for a moment, uncertain if it was the twilight of dawn or dusk. Her stomach was tight, as if she were upset about something.

"Oh, no," she gasped out loud.

There was a rustle. "…'wake, Miss?" said Jane's voice.

"Yes."

It took Kitty a second to gather why Jane was there. Jane must be sleeping in the chair to keep her company.

"You're good to me, Jane," she whispered.

"You've got good taste in books," said Jane in a satisfied voice. "Now go back to sleep. Dreadful things are best faced after a full night's sleep."

"Do you happen to know if it's within the law for a man to whip his sister?" Kitty said glumly the next morning.

"Don't know, Miss," said Jane doubtfully, "but remember you can move faster than him."

Kitty wiggled with discomfort as Jane adjusted the laces of the stays the upstairs maid had loaned her. Hers had been washed but weren't yet dry enough to wear.

The upstairs maid was almost, but not quite her size. Kitty forced herself to be still, feeling that the stiff boning digging into her armpit was the least of the tortures she deserved.

If she hadn't brought Louisa here, Bastable wouldn't have come. John wouldn't have been shot. He wouldn't be in danger… of…perhaps….

Without even stopping to drink a cup of tea, she made to go downstairs as as soon as she was dressed. She cast a glance at Louisa's door in passing it.

She *couldn't*. Not yet. She didn't know what to say.

She supposed she was angry—but it was a flat, cold feeling in her heart: rather than what she felt when she thought of Bastable, which was hot and white. If *he* had shown his face right then, she would have punched him in the nose.

She took two steps down the stairs and then turned and went back up.

If—when—she argued with Ned, she would be committing herself to a line of decision. She needed to have it out with Louisa first.

She knocked sharply on Louisa's door with a knuckle. The white flash of her own hand startled her. She looked at it. That hand had been all slick and bloody yesterday. There were little raw spots on her fingers. Jane had scrubbed fiercely under her fingernails.

She crossed her arms, feeling cold and unsteady.

"Louisa, it's Kitty. Let me in."

"We'll go away," said Louisa tonelessly, looking at her hands in her lap. "Today. Don't worry."

She looked up then. Her expression was pinched and her eyes dark with want of sleep.

"Kitty, given the evils I've brought upon your family, I don't know if this means anything to you. But I'll say it regardless. You've been kinder to me than anyone I've ever known. And your brothers are—" her mouth worked as she looked for the word. "Gallant."

"Yes, they are, aren't they," said Kitty without inflection. "Tell me something."

"What is that?"

"When you said you'd marry Bastable. Why?"

"I didn't say I'd marry him. I said I'd go with him."

"All right. Why?"

Louisa looked at her, unblinking. "To get him away from you. If he'd come here once, he'd come again."

"You didn't intend to marry him?"

Louisa hesitated. "I thought perhaps...." Then, abruptly: "—No. At *that* point—before everything else that happened—I could have been his mistress. Even if that meant I was always a breath from being cast off into the gutter." She spoke very coolly, as if talking about someone else. "But I could not stand up in church before God and take his name and be his forever. I'd rather die."

Kitty sat back and looked at her in silence.

Finally, she said: "You may not go. I don't know how much I can love you right now; and if Mr Stanger dies I don't know if I'll ever forgive either of us. But I do know you owe my brother thanks. And we both, I think, owe Mr Stanger an apology."

Louisa looked at her with her face so white Kitty was afraid she might faint.

"You told me once you nursed your parents before they died," said Kitty. "I imagine that Ned will want to stay with him at all hours, even at the expense of his own health. I could use some help."

"Where is my brother?" Kitty asked Howard when they met him in the staircase hall. The butler also looked short on sleep.

"Mr Fairwell is with Mr Stanger in the Italian room."

"If we offer our services as nurses, are we likely to get anything thrown at us?" Kitty asked directly.

Howard's lips twitched, although no smile touched his eyes. He hesitated for a second. "May I suggest requesting an audience with Mr Stanger in specific? It seems unlikely Mr Fairwell would dare attack someone else's guest."

"Do you know if Mr Stanger is awake?"

"As of a few minutes ago, yes."

Feeling ridiculous, Kitty said: "Would you be so kind as to announce us?"

Howard raised his eyebrows slightly but he went to the door of the Italian room and rapped on it.

Kitty followed a few yards back. Louisa huddled behind her, clutching her hand.

There was a muffled, Ned-like sound from within the room. Howard stuck his head inside the room.

Kitty could hear what he said: "Miss Fairwell and Miss Green request Mr Stanger's permission to to enter."

"Miss Fairwell and Miss Green can go to hell!" shouted Ned.

Howard waited another second, clearly listening to Mr Stanger's response, which Kitty couldn't hear. "Thank you, sir; a moment."

He withdrew his head and closed the door. He looked down at Kitty. "Tread softly, Miss Fairwell. I believe Mr Stanger has bought you a few seconds."

*

So this was the Italian room.

There was nothing Italian about it. It was dark blue and packed with the assorted items of a bachelor's life and work, even further disarrayed when the room had been rapidly turned into a sickroom. A desk to her left; a table shoved half in front of the fireplace to the right, where it clearly didn't go. Paperwork and books and news-papers and mismatched chairs and a hunting gun broken down and a muddy greatcoat and a tray with some tea and nibbled bread.

The bed holding John Stanger, lying on his side under a sheet, had its headboard under the window across the room from her.

Ned was in a chair by his friend's head, looking across the room at the two of them like an adder staring at rats. Kitty wished she could sink through the floor rather than continue to exist under that gaze.

"They're *my* visitors, Ned, don't scare them off," said John Stanger in a weak but clear voice. "Pardon me for not getting up, ladies…."

Kitty smiled with a quiver in her lip.

"Do me a favour and come up here, won't you?" whispered Mr Stanger. "I haven't got eyes in my feet."

This meant getting nearer to Ned, who was still giving them a deadly stare. Kitty gave him a level gaze that was a complete lie.

In order to stand where Mr Stanger could easily see them, Kitty had to hover within swiping distance of Ned's cane. On an impulse, tugging Louisa along with her, she got down on the floor in front of Mr Stanger so they could see eye to eye. She had expected him to be lying on his stomach, but instead he was propped up on his side by pillows. He was dreadfully pale.

"Hullo Kitty," he said softly.

Oh *dear*.

Kitty smelled brandy. Well, that made sense, he would be in awful pain, but at the same time Ned was *right there*. Her skirt was practically touching Ned's boot. She prayed that he chalked Mr Stanger's using her Christian name down to general mental muddle.

"Th-thank you for seeing us, Mr Stanger. We're—fully aware that if we hadn't come to Gatewood, Bastable wouldn't have come and y-you wouldn't have been shot. So if you're angry that's completely fair, of course, but still we would like to—well, it seems likely Ned is going to *want* to stay with you all the time, but he needs to sleep sometimes. So if you need company whilst he sleeps, either of us can do that."

He smiled at her. "Too drunk to be mad. P'raps later." When he was drunk he sounded less Oxbridge and more Leicester. "Yes, please keep me company. I'd love it. You know why?"

"Why?" Kitty asked warily.

"Because if I die there'll be a two out of three chance the last face I saw was a pretty girl."

"HA!" snorted Ned, giving his cane a little punctuation clack against the floor.

"And that's so much better than most men get!" John finished.

Kitty smiled with a quivering mouth. She slid her eyes over to Ned's knees and then up to his face. His chin was propped on his hand. He looked haggard.

On impulse, she stood up and leaned down and kissed him on his bald spot. He gave a start.

"I love you and I'm sorry," said Kitty softly, her hand on his cheek. He hadn't shaved.

He just snorted again. But he didn't argue.

That might be the best she'd get for a while. Until they found out if John was going to live or die.

"Did you eat some breakfast?" she asked.

"Don't start managing me, woman," said Ned.

"Oh yes you should," said John from the bed in a barely audible voice. "Us'ly my job, y'know?"

CHAPTER TWELVE

EARLY THE NEXT MORNING, Thomas the footman was able to provide Kitty's desired intelligence. Mr Fairwell and Mr Stanger had vehemently refused to call a doctor on the grounds of considering all of them quacks. John Quire, whose last employer had it seemed been an inveterate dueller, had agreed. He himself was now down-stairs having breakfast.

Kitty fretted over the decision. If they didn't call a doctor and Mr Stanger died, mightn't they be partly to blame?

Still, Ned and he both had significantly more experience with doctors than she had. She supposed that if they were in agreement they were probably right.

She would do what *was* within her power. Right now that meant endeavouring not to worry too much about Mr Stanger, and seeing to it that *Ned* was able to rest.

She went with Louisa to the saloon with the intention of quickly eating a few bites to get up her strength before chasing Ned back to his own couch.

It was in that circumstance that she had the misfortune of coming across Miss Horne.

She was, of course, already well-acquainted with Miss Horne, as the guardian and chaperon of her friend.

She was always generously, immaculately polite to Miss Horne.

Not just for Louisa's sake, but also for the particular reason that Kitty found Miss Horne revolting.

Miss Horne's age was hard to guess. The black hair visible around the edges of her lace cap had no grey in it, but her pinched, puckered mouth was lined and her hands were bony. Kitty did not think her want of attractiveness was due to any physical sign of age —Mrs Wolcott was older but still had much charm—but rather due to a stinginess of spirit, as if she would refuse on principal to admit that sugar was sweet.

There was also something bothersome about her nose. Kitty had spent too much time analysing what it was, when forced to make conversation with her and trying to distract herself from her voice. The outside rim of Miss Horne's nostrils curved up with a swoop like the angle of an ice skate's blade, thus failing to do its job of keeping the interior strictly interior. In viewing the lady's nose from even the slightest side angle, one felt rather unfortunately that one was looking straight into Miss Horne's skull.

Kitty had always been sure that Miss Horne had good qualities. One of these days, she had always believed, she would discover one, and all of this being appallingly genteel would be *worth* it.

She was not so sure of that any more. Miss Horne was responsible for bringing Bastable into this house. And therefore, directly, for John Stanger's being shot.

Seeing Miss Horne seated in the saloon at breakfast, Kitty stopped in the doorway. Miss Horne saw her and at once stood. A sickly smile stuck onto her face.

"Miss Fairwell!"

Kitty looked her in the eye, and realized at the last second that if she spoke, she'd scream.

Instead she did what it had never occurred to her she'd ever do: she turned around and walked out again.

She dashed up the stairs, shaking, praying neither Miss Horne nor Louisa would follow her.

It was possible that since their eye contact had been so brief, Miss Horne would be in doubt as to whether Kitty had given her the cut direct. That was probably good. At some point, Kitty might be forced by circumstances to be civil to her again. A cut direct couldn't be taken back. But to undertake it was also more of a clear, deliberate thing—of resolutely ignoring someone's address before witnesses. In this case, her abrupt exit could be excused by stress and distraction.

Perhaps that was, in essence, even true.

Kitty was going to leave it for later. In the meantime, she was going to ring for some tea and toast in her room, collect materials to resume her neglected letter-writing, and return downstairs posthaste to take over Ned's watch.

No one answered, ten minutes later, when she knocked on the door of the Italian room—first lightly and then, after a moment passed, more strongly. But she thought she heard—was that a snore? After another moment, she dared open it and peeked inside.

The reason for the lack of response was immediately evident. Ned had fallen asleep in the chair, his head tipped back. As she stood in the door, he emitted a monstrous snore.

"Who's there?" said John feebly. "Will you get this oaf out of here? He's keeping me awake."

The door that connected the Italian room with the library was to her advantage when it came to getting her refractory brother shifted to his couch; he had barely to move twenty steps. Once he was in the library, Kitty watched him through the doorway to be certain that he was indeed lying down. He was, with a groan.

"Awaken me if there's the slightest sign of fever," he demanded.

"I promise," said Kitty truthfully.

She knew that had their positions been reversed she would have rested much more soundly hearing a promise.

She closed the door and sat in the chair Ned had been in. It was still cosily warm. Mr Stanger lay directly to her left beneath the window. She glanced over at him; his eyes were closed. Very well, she thought. Now, Kitty Fairwell, you will test your patience.

She rose as quietly as possible, took up the lap desk one of the servants had found for her, and settled down to write letters. It was going to take her a long time to find the right words.

*

"Writing to a beau?" John said softly when she was in the middle of letter number three.

She was putting Percy's letter off to last. She felt it was terribly unfair of her. It was merely that things like gunshot wounds didn't fit into the conversations she'd had with Percy. If he'd talked about someone's war wound or a hunting accident, she probably would have covered her ears and jested, "Oh, no, don't tell me about it!" as a young lady was supposed to do.

In any event, she was not writing to him when Mr Stanger made his inquiry. She wiped her pen and her fingers on a rag and set her lap desk on the floor. "To my sister Susannah. How do you feel?"

"Like I've got a big hole in my back," he said frankly. "Imagine a hot poker held in Satan's cloven hoof."

"I'm surprised you're on your side like that. Wouldn't you be more comfortable on your stomach?"

"A wound like that has to drain. Did you really get the bullet out?"

"Yes."

"Let me see your fingers."

His head was pillowed toward her on his right hand, but it seemed he could still move his left through a small degree of motion without too much pain, because he wiggled his fingers at her. She held out her hand.

"Oh—" she said when he caught it and moved it where he could examine it "—it's inky…." Her heart was going wild.

He ran his fingers over hers as if judging their suitability from digging bullets out of his back. Kitty found it unbearably erotic, and quite unfair. He had a serious expression and had to be unaware of the effect he was having. He pulled her hand a little closer and kissed the back of it, featherlight, in an un-inky spot. Then he let go.

Kitty drew back. She looked at the closed library door behind her. She couldn't believe she was going to say this. She reached back and covered the keyhole firmly with her thumb.

"I can't say it was at all how I imagined getting under your shirt,

Mr Stanger," she whispered.

His un-brow shot up. He exhaled a single "ha!" and then his face curled up in pain. "Damn. Don't make me laugh."

"I'm sorry." She looked at him, resisting with all her might the desire to kiss him. Blessedly, a memory cooled the desire.

She cleared her throat. "Since I'm writing letters, would you like me to send a note to your young woman for you?"

"My what?" he said, startled, and then abruptly, "Oh." He caught his breath like it hurt. He looked down, away from her eyes. "She's marrying the blacksmith, and best of luck to her."

"Oh," said Kitty shakily, "that's dreadful. I'm sorry."

It was in essence true. She couldn't imagine what sort of mad-woman would turn down John Stanger. She hated to think of his being pained by it.

"Well then," she said after a moment, "is there anything else I can do?"

"No, I'm—" He paused for a moment and then flicked his eyes up again. "Ah, what the hell. I want a kiss. I mean, I've been wanting one for a while. But it seems more urgent now—before the fever sets in and I'm too busy wondering if I'm going to make it—"

Kitty shivered. "How long does that usually take?"

"A day or three." His eyes pled with her.

He didn't need to plead; she didn't need an excuse.

Kitty knelt on the floor, then found it put her too low. She put her hand on the bed and leaned forward. He still smelled a little bit like brandy.

She brushed his lips with hers. Oh, that, she could see the appeal of that. He was so hot it seemed he warmed the very air. She sat back on her heels, still braced with one hand on the bed. It hadn't been enough. She leaned forward again, adjusting her position to avoid hitting his nose. Then for some reason he parted his lips a little. That seemed like a good idea.

Later, she thought, I will have a chance to talk myself out of this. Not right now.

"If you stay alive," she said, "you get a kiss every day."

He smiled, obviously in intense pain. "I'll stay alive forever, then."

She sat back into the chair, trying to smile.

"You know that when I asked if there was anything else I could do, I meant a sip of water. Or writing a letter for you."

"Ah well," he said ruefully, "aiming too low has never been a failing of mine."

"You should sleep."

John Quire checked in at intervals. At midday, Kitty was chased out.

Louisa spelled her for the afternoon. Avoiding Miss Horne, Kitty stole a book from the library and hid in her room.

She wished Will were here! He would know how to deal with Miss Horne. And he would natter nervously about something ridiculous, which would keep her from this terrible thing she was doing—*thinking*.

"Please God, let Mr Stanger make a full recovery" seemed a dreadfully childish prayer, yet she couldn't manage to form anything better.

He did have a fever that night, though Kitty only found out about it from Jane the following morning. As soon as Kitty was told, a shiver crept down her back, as if she herself were taking ill.

She met John Quire as he was leaving the Italian room.

"How—how—" she stammered.

He shrugged phlegmatically. "It's draining about as well as you'd hope. Bit of chills. Get your brother to sleep."

When she went in, Ned said something rude to her, but toneless.

"That's all very well," she said with only a little tremor, "but I imagine you've been up all night, so go lie down."

"Ye-s-s," said Mr Stanger, shivering, "the quality of your c-conversation goes quite d-downhill when you haven't had enough sleep.

P'raps you'll be b-better, Miss Fairwell."

Ned looked at him and touched his hand and then took himself off. Kitty took his warm seat again.

It seemed not right to ask him how he felt; his face was flushed and sweaty and she could hear his teeth chattering. "I'm sorry to hear you aren't doing so well today," she said in a little voice.

"Me t-too. G-glad to see you though. How long do I have to make it before I get that k-kiss? D-determined not to m-miss out."

Kitty moved forward and kissed him much more lightly than yesterday as he was shivering. She made herself smile at him. "If you're doing well enough to ask for a kiss I suppose I shouldn't worry too much."

"Not too b-bad yet. The unf-fair thing is," he said, "every t-time I'm dying I'm aware of it."

"How many times have you been dying?" Kitty exclaimed.

"Twice. Three times. Depends on how you count. 'Flu when I was a kid. My sister had it and was r-raving nonsense, and I lay there in the sick room listening to her, staring at the ceiling wishing I could just go off my head like she did."

"Second time—" he hesitated. "Nah, that doesn't count. N-next time was when I was in hospital after Albuera. Nicked by a F-frenchy's blade across my collarbone. It turned the worst colours and I lay there shivering like a leaf, miserable beyond belief and just waiting forever an' ever. So here we go, round three. At least now I've got good c-company."

He swallowed. She offered him some water which he sipped with the help of a fat hollow piece of straw. He had to shift a little to drink, and settling back down he groaned.

"Don't talk, I can see it pains you."

"Breathing hurts and I've g-got to do that. Might as well talk. Need a distraction."

"I'm so angry at myself that we came here," Kitty whispered. "This is all my fault. I'm so sorry."

"Ha, ha. That's what Miss Green said too. Going to tell you

what I told her. It's that grandling bastard's fault for trying to shoot the door open. To abduct a girl!

"An' her fault, some, for getting in his bed to start with, but she couldn't have known *this*. But certainly Miss Horne's fault for bringing him here and 'specially shame on her for wanting her ward to marry a man with fast fists.

"May be Ned's fault a bit, for making Miss Green write to Miss Horne wi'out making sure she had her best interests in mind.

"But I don't see how it's *your* fault for coming here to get away from the blackguard to start with. It was pretty good sense, I think."

She understood, and his words should have lightened her soul, but they didn't. "Ned blames me," she whispered. "Please don't die, for his sake. He would j-just be d-destroyed. I couldn't bear another person—" She stopped. "Oh, please just work hard at not dying. That's all."

"Who've you lost, Miss Fairwell?" he asked softly.

It took her a second to understand he'd mistaken her meaning. She stumbled looking for an answer. "Oh, n-no, I— I've been lucky. No one really close to me. We had a cousin whose wife was beheaded by the French—and Robert lost an arm. And, ah, Susannah's husband is not well at all, but— But I've only lost my mother and that doesn't count as I didn't know her. Oh dear," she added dully. "Do you really want to know? It seems like we should talk about something more pleasant."

"Why?" he said.

"It just seems to me—if you're ill, it's better to keep to conversation that keeps your spirits up."

"Or you could just tell me why you're sniffling."

"Oh—well—I just had this awfully selfish thought…" It came out against her better judgment. "If you die then Ned will look at me and think *You killed my best friend*. And I couldn't bear it. Because already sometimes I feel Papa looks at me and thinks *You killed my wife*. I look like her and, and, it's so unfair. I *don't* know why any of them were ever surprised I was desperate to get out of that house!"

She wiped her eyes on her palms, trying to control herself. She gulped. "I suppose you're going to tell Ned. It's all right, as long as you make him swear not to tell Papa. Not that I think he would, but —just in case. I'm so sorry, I *warned* you it was a selfish thought. P-please forget I spoke."

"You're *not* telling me your father b-blames you for your mother's death," he said sharply.

"No, not—anything he ever said. He's always been so sweet to me. But he is sad, and I can—see it when he looks at me, sometimes, and he gets so quiet I can't bear it."

"Don't you think he's thinking he's so grateful to have you?" he said, still sharp. "So grateful he didn't lose you too? You were your mother's gift to him. By God, Kitty, my daughter died and I would give anything in the world to have her back."

"Oh! You—I didn't know you had a daughter."

"Plenty of women die the way your mother did," he said in a flat voice, "so did Maria. And it wasn't Cora's fault, was it; we wanted children and there's always that risk. So if it isn't gratitude your father's feeling when he looks at you—then to hell with him."

"N-no, I—" She couldn't say anything more, not in response to that.

Something funny had turned over in her chest. Well, perhaps *to hell with him* was right. Or perhaps she'd been wrong. She would have to try those thoughts on for size, in private, or perhaps the next time she went to Grandbourne.

She leaned forward and took his hand and squeezed. She could feel the tremble of his chills, passing in waves. "I'm so awfully sorry."

"Me too. But it was a long time ago."

"*Now* can we talk about something more pleasant," she said tremulously, "unless you want to sleep?"

He sighed. "I've just slept all night and if I lie staring at the quilt I'll start to think too much. But you'll have to lead the conversation. I don't know what ladies talk about."

"Mostly very dull things," said Kitty, thinking of the Misses Wolcott. She blushed. Where had that come from?

"Will you tell me about Leicestershire?" she said. "I've never been."

He groaned. "It's sheep on one side, politics on the other, and stockings tying them together. All love to my family, but I don't like sheep or politics, so I'm glad I'm rid of the place."

But he told her about growing up in a draper's shop in Leicester, and his family for whom he had great affection, and the politics of making stockings, until he drifted off to sleep. He was shivering less, and she hoped it was over with.

The next day he was worse.

No chills now, just a raging fever, but as he'd said, he never went off his head. When Kitty at last gained admittance, he opened tired eyes just long enough to smile at her with false bravado.

Ned refused to leave him at all; then finally gave in and went for an hour's rest, provided John Quire stayed with him.

So John Stanger didn't get today's kiss—she didn't dare, not with John Quire reading the newspaper six feet away. But when she wiped his face with water, she pressed two fingers against his burning-hot lips. He smiled and closed his eyes again.

Those were some bad days. Especially once he stopped being able to make conversation.

Kitty slept and dressed and ate and read the letters that came back in return for her own, but mostly she was willing him not to die with all the power of her heart. Sometimes she sat on the floor next to Ned, in long hours of silence broken by fitful noises from John.

Other people's lives went on, to her irritation. Miss Horne tried to ambush her in the upstairs hall.

"I'm terribly sorry," said Kitty with detachment, "it's possible you may be responsible for killing my brother's best friend. I suggest you don't talk to me until we find out if it's so."

Miss Horne started to make a noise of a protest, but she wasn't stupid. She started avoiding Kitty.

Louisa also was taking shifts at John's bedside. Always quiet, she now spoke almost not at all. Ned didn't mention her to Kitty once. Kitty tried to think clearly about it. He had been so vehement that Kitty end her association with Louisa; that Louisa be cast out as soon as possible. But then, in front of almost the whole household, he had ripped up her marriage license with utterly clear contempt for Harry Bastable.

Ned had many flaws but Kitty did not think hypocrisy was among them. If he had demonstrated that he did not truly think Louisa should have married Bastable, he could hardly turn about and say that she'd been wrong to flee from him.

Or perhaps he considered her a useful nurse, and he was tolerating her to be used and ignored until she was no longer necessary.

Or perhaps—most likely—he just didn't care any more. He only cared about John.

John Tickle came by one bright morning when Kitty was trying to get Ned to go to bed.

Mr Tickle said he was quite sorry about Mr Stanger, and he hoped he'd be on his feet again soon. The problem was, Wilkie Rye and Tom Beadle were arguing again. *This* time it was one-or-the-other-of-em's chickens.

Kitty saw all colour drain out of Ned's face. Of necessity, he'd been moving around more than usual, and she had already been able to see that he was in a great deal of pain.

Words came out of her from nowhere. "Are these the fellows who weren't sure whose pig it was, last week?"

"Aye, that's them."

"And they live about about a five mile ride down bad lanes?"

"Sorry to say it."

"I'll go," Kitty said calmly, feeling the strangest sort of dignity.

John Tickle said, "*You?*" but Ned just looked down at her.

No, the words hadn't come from nowhere. She was, like it or not, her father's daughter.

"Believe it or not, Mr Tickle," Kitty said, addressing him but looking levelly up at Ned, "I'm not a stranger to arguments about livestock. But, more to the point, they're not going to argue with *me*. They wouldn't dare."

When she looked over her shoulder, she found John Tickle with his hat in hand, grinning. "You might be right, Miss."

John Tickle returned her that afternoon. Ned stuck his head out of the library door whilst she was still trying to get out the boots loaned to her by Mrs Dowell (who had remarkably tiny feet for a woman of her proportion).

Kitty leaned on Adam, hopping. The footman had gone along with her, wearing something more nondescript than a footman's livery.

"Well?" Ned said brusquely. Then, "Adam, did you—bring back one of the chickens?"

Kitty had spent an hour to settle the dispensation of the last chicken.

"It's broth for Mr Stanger," she said, "and in exchange for a chicken every fortnight, we're going to build them a better fence; and if they don't maintain the fence I'm going to make the vicar start a school and send them to it so they can keep better records."

Ned digested this. "The vicar's opposed to a school."

"Is he? Then I'll go talk to the Methodists. Being shown up by them might change his tune."

Ned said "HA!"

And then: "He's still asleep, but I think his fever's broken."

*

Later, when Mr Stanger was awake and hungry and complaining about Ned's conversation again, she fed him the broth from the chicken and told him how she'd come by it.

He wheezed with laughter. "I told you not to make me laugh! Kitty Fairwell versus Wilkie Rye and Tom Beadle in the farmyard! I would give everything I own to have seen that."

He looked over at her and she wasn't greatly skilled at reading *I adore you* in a man's eyes, but she had the terrifying feeling that was it.

Chapter Thirteen

THEY TOLD HIM HE'D MISSED five days. What an astonishing thing—he hadn't noticed them go by. He was rather pleased by it.

John Quire, who helped him with his necessities and examined his back a few times a day, said bluntly that he wasn't out of the woods yet. "It looks better, though. I might bandage it up soon."

"Oh, good—"

"Of course, y'might still die of lockjaw."

John groaned. "I appreciate your good cheer, as always."

When Ned brought him dinner, displacing Miss Green who had been reading him yesterday's newspaper in a low clear voice, John waited for him to get settled down in his chair.

"So Kitty's taking my job, is she?" said John.

Ned snorted. "What did she tell you?"

"Well, she *didn't* say she had them eating out of her hand—but I can read between the lines."

"Kitty can be very charming," said Ned grudgingly. "It's good to see her using her brain for once, instead of wasting it on dresses and dreams of riding carriages in Hyde Park."

John was suddenly regretting having started this line of conversation, even if it had seemed amusing at first. He didn't want to talk about Kitty to Ned. He especially didn't want to think about Kitty promenading in Hyde Park amongst the *haut ton*. If John dared set foot in Hyde Park they'd consider him barely better than riffraff.

"You ever ridden a carriage in Hyde Park?" he asked Ned amiably. "May be it's worth dreaming about."

"Robert dragged me a few times. On horse, not driving. It was cold and crowded and we couldn't ride twenty feet without getting talked at by some matron who wanted us for sons-in-law. Robert thought it was hilarious."

"Ah, dreadful problem to have."

John had no interest in the questionable charms of Hyde Park, full, as it was, of people who would look down their noses at him.

But perhaps it was good to think of it often—as a reminder of the irreconcilable distance between Kitty and himself. It sent a violent *twang* through his chest like a snapping rope. And that was good, because when she talked about chickens and kept him apprised of the state of the turnips, he found himself thinking things like, *When I'm well, I'll*—

He'd learned this lesson. He had. He'd tried to overreach himself before, and been miserable. Ned had rescued him, thank God, by asking for help, and making him realize that the only reason he was sticking by a mistake was hard-headed pride. Selling his commission and coming to Gatewood House had been a relief beyond his imaginings.

It certainly hadn't been *easy*, dealing with Ned in the beginning, and not knowing much about farming. But good nature and a quick brain could accomplish things here. They'd been to very little avail when dealing with a pack of titled officers.

Men like him should aim for women like Molly Weaver.

Perhaps, when he could get around again, he should find some other woman in the village and pay her proper court. And not mind so much if he only *liked* her.

Or perhaps he should take a subscription to the dances at the nearest Assembly Rooms. He'd either need to stay in town, or go only when the moon was full enough to travel home by. But that was all right; Ned didn't need him all the time anymore. It was a fine idea. He'd do it.

By plenty of women's standards, he'd be a good catch.

As soon as his back healed, and Miss Fairwell left....

And assuming he didn't die of lockjaw, of course....

Was it any surprise that dreaming of Kitty Fairwell (here in his bed, to be frank—not in Hyde Park) was so tempting, when all other immediate possibilities involved terrible ways to die?

*

Now that he was conscious again, they were such long days. He slept some during the day, and lay awake some at night, but he was always awake in the mornings for Kitty.

They didn't flirt with each other, not really. Perhaps it was just the knowledge that Ned was slumbering (or not) directly in the next room, and whilst the doors had never felt thin before, Kitty would glance at it sometimes, and John knew what she was thinking. An inadvertent chaperon.

So they talked about ordinary things—farming; and where she might find some additional maids (he didn't comment how she seemed to be taking over as mistress of the house); and Napoleon, because everything always came back to Napoleon.

But the look in her eyes wasn't ordinary. She always turned the chair so they could converse, face-to-face. As they spoke he felt her gaze on him like a touch, fixing intently on his eyes and then stroking across his lips; lingering on his hair as if she wished it would fall out of its ribbon; brushing across his chest hidden beneath his linen shirt. She was unaware of her own look, he was certain of it; her conversation didn't falter and there was never anything even slightly provocative about her *words*.

Just that gaze.

He was grateful for shirt and blanket and the pillows, which bolstered him onto his side but also hid the reaction he had to her closeness. If he could feel her gaze on his naked skin he would have begged her to come into the bed with him.

Sometimes—perhaps she was unconscious of it—she would lean forward with her elbows on her knees, unladylike in the extreme, as if she wished she *could* get just a little closer. The neckline of her dress revealed a hint of ripe curves—oh, yes, he looked—but not anywhere near enough. Nothing compared to what a dancing partner at a ball would have seen down the low-cut bodice of the finest evening gown.

But not a single word that couldn't be uttered with easy conscience in front of her brothers.

Though she asked him once, apropos of nothing, in a low voice with a tremor as if she were breaking a resolution: "May I ask why you wear your hair long? I don't know if it's old-fashioned—or so fashionable Brummell hasn't yet caught up to you."

"Do you want to know my secret, Miss Fairwell?"

She leaned forward, hardly breathing.

"I am *vain*," he whispered. She giggled. And then, in a normal tone, he added: "But not fashionable. If I were fashionable I'd try to make it curl."

"No, you mustn't! I don't understand why people who don't have curls try to get them; they never do what you want them to. They are a *bane*."

He wanted to tell her how beautiful she was. Her bright dancing grey eyes, her wild chestnut hair, her soft lips. How perfectly small and delicate she was, but full in the places where it mattered.

Instead, he made himself ask her about what the London season was like. Her voice was merry as she told him about turtle soup with a viscount as her dinner companion (all he could talk about was his gout); drinking negus at one in the morning after hours of dancing; the hypocrisies of the Almack's mistresses; and yes, driving in Hyde Park. He smiled to invite her to go on, and almost welcomed the pain in his back, because it helped balance out the pain in his chest.

"Are you afraid you'll miss the end of it?"

"Oh, well; Parliament doesn't close until the third week of July. There's plenty of time." And then, "No. I'd rather be here."

Once a day she kissed him. Just once. And then she sat in the chair and they didn't touch again.

When, once a day, she leaned toward him and they tasted each other, he wouldn't let himself so much as brush his fingers across her arm. If he did, then he would want more, and he couldn't do more, not with a hole in his back. Jostling it open would mean it would take even longer to heal.

The sooner it healed, the sooner he could tug her onto the bed with him, tuck his arm around her trim waist, bury his nose in her curls, feel her warm breath against his neck.

No, no. He couldn't do that.

"Miss Green," he said.

She lowered the newspaper. "Yes, Mr Stanger."

She had the most colourless voice, like glass. And her face was always clear of emotion. He could never tell what she was thinking.

"Would you be offended if I ask you a personal question? *I* won't be offended if you don't care to answer, of course."

That got the slightest expression out of her. Her brow knit. "You may ask."

"Do you think it's better to regret something you do, or something you don't?"

She was silent a long time.

Finally she said, in her quiet way, "I don't know, Mr Stanger. Except for what part I played in your injury, I regret nothing."

She picked up the newspaper again. "Perhaps I am wicked. Or perhaps that answers your question."

Ned crossed paths with Miss Green, insofar as John could tell, for no more than the ten seconds each day in which Ned and John Quire were coming into the Italian room, and she was rising to go out. She always kept her head down and said nothing more than "Good night, sir."

The trouble was she was a tall young lady, and breathtakingly beautiful. Keeping her head down didn't hide it.

At first John had thought that Ned was avoiding looking at her because he was pretending she didn't exist. Then he intercepted a second, brief glance when her back was turned. John stowed that for discussion when they were alone.

Finally John Quire went away, and Ned settled down. There was a lamp on the small table just beside his chair, and John could make out his face.

With his usable hand John very carefully forked up a small piece of veal from the plate Ned had settled on the bed in front of him. Before he put it in his mouth he said:

"Did you and Miss Fairwell ever decide what to do about Miss Green?"

Ned made a short growling noise. "I have enough to deal with. Frequently I think of sending her and Miss Horne packing, but—"

"—but?" John prompted with his mouth full.

"But it's Kitty's problem, and I'm through with any attempts to fix her problems for her."

"Did you ever find out exactly what their situation was?"

"They've got about 20*l.* per annum put together."

The maids each got about 6*l.* a year, and that was generous pay. But they also received room and board and clothing.

"Oof. I can see why Miss Horne might think her better off married to a piece of work like Bastable."

"Well, I don't," said Ned. "But like I said, Kitty's problem. When she goes, they go. So I am ignoring the matter."

"A sophisticated choice, my friend."

"My ignoring things is working well for everyone at the moment," Ned said shortly.

John looked at him. So he did know.

It wasn't him who'd let fall any hint. He'd only slipped once, perhaps, or twice, saying "Kitty" rather than "Miss Fairwell." But that was what *Ned* called her, so he felt it was excusable.

And of course, what *was* he ignoring? What did he believe? That Kitty…fancied John? The reverse? He could deny everything. John, too, could ignore Ned's unstated implication. And they could go on as they had been.

God, he wanted to tell him. He hated having a secret from Ned; it felt like an unnatural weight, nagging him every time they spoke.

And, too, Ned could help him. He could help him end it cleanly, by doing something so simple as putting Kitty on a carriage to London, or to Grandbourne.

Would you follow her? he thought, unbidden. Lord. He was afraid he would follow her. He was afraid he would ask her to elope with him.

Since when did he become the kind of man who would do *that*, rather than just having the vicar read banns like anyone else?

She might laugh at him. No, she wouldn't. She would say, My father's not going to deny me marrying you. You saved Ned's life, after all.

He had the sense that the problem wouldn't be Patrick Fairwell, and any expectations he might have for his daughter. It was just... the difference between party slippers and muddy boots.

He wanted her to be his—but he couldn't change the way life was just by wanting it. She had been presented to the Queen as a debutante.

"What do you and my sister talk about?" Ned asked, as if he wasn't sure he wanted to.

John *wasn't* Miss Green—with no regrets. *Her* life was in ruins.

"Well," said John, "Yesterday, we were talking about cheese."

"Cheese."

"Naturally, I hold that Leicestershire makes the best cheese. *She* insists that French cheese is the best. Soft cheese with a bad smell. I'm not sure I understand the appeal. I suppose being invited to fancy parties ruins you for the beauty of good, crumbly, orange, English cheese."

Ned thought about it in silence.

"I might have said the same, two months ago," he said at last, "but I don't think so anymore. I think you've been a good influence on her."

John had no idea what to say to that. As far as he could tell, he'd mostly been a bad, bad influence on Kitty Fairwell.

Ned's gaze was fixed on the far wall across John's bed. "I may be speaking out of turn," he said slowly, "and forgive me; you know I've never been a diplomatic man."

Oh hell, thought John.

Ned said, simply, "I'd be delighted if you married Kitty."

A passionate joy shot through John. He wasn't, after the first second, foolish enough to think that was the only, or even one of the main important things. But hearing it spoken by his friend made him want to weep with gratitude.

"You do me an honour," he said very softly.

Ned smiled, very briefly, still not looking at him. "It's purely selfish. God knows I don't want to deal with some *ton* fop." Then he continued. "Susannah, on the other hand, may feel differently. She has three daughters who are going to need marrying off. She's always—mostly—been respectable. And Kitty looks up to her."

John had to make some response, so he made a nondescript sound of acknowledgment. His head and his heart were too full.

"As a brother," Ned said, still not looking at him, "it also behooves me to note that if you get her with child, I'll kill you."

"Ah—" John wanted to protest that it wasn't like that.

Except inside his head.

He said wryly: "Duly noted."

"Good." Ned moved his head, looking toward the table. Still not at John. John smiled. A brave man and a loud one, but also crushingly shy at times.

"Did Miss Green read you the newspaper already?"

It didn't make it easier, knowing Ned's opinion. It didn't answer the question John had been asking himself:

Would Kitty be happy with me?

The next morning Kitty came in when Ned and John Quire were leaving. When she sat and smiled at him with her slippered feet neatly beside each other, he saw something was different; there was a tension in the smile that hadn't been there yesterday.

"Good morning, Mr Stanger, how are you today?"

"Faring well, Miss Fairwell."

He didn't tease Ned about their family name, but it amused Kitty.

She had taken the habit of telling him what the morning was like—he could see some sky through his window but he liked to hear what sort of birds were about, and how the fields were coming along (some of them could be seen from Kitty's room upstairs) and whether there were any clouds to remark on.

"It sounds very fine, Miss Fairwell."

Some days, she waited to kiss him. It almost meant more then, for it was never an afterthought, but something he could see her thinking about, until she could resist no more. On those days when she waited he tried to make her laugh, because that seemed to break down her resistance to temptation.

Today she was already looking at him with heated eyes. She slipped out of her chair, moved forward the one necessary step, and put her hand on the mattress to find the right awkward position.

She touched her lips to his. He didn't draw back, but he hesitated.

She pulled away at once. She sat on her heels beside the bed and examined his face. "Are you all right?" she asked, sounding frightened. "Does your back hurt?"

"No, it's healing well." He smiled with hooded eyes. "John Quire even went so far as to bandage it."

"But that's—very good, isn't it?"

"It is good. I'll have to try sitting up soon—there will be a time when it's better to stretch it, than not."

"But then why—" She stopped abruptly.

He was watching her face. "Do *you* know why?"

She spoke unwillingly. "Ned said something, didn't he."

John said softly: "How did he know?"

"I don't know." She tugged a stray curl. "Really, I don't. I think it was something very ordinary. Yesterday when I saw him, he said, 'How was John this morning?' and I-I—think I smiled. Shouldn't it be all right to smile when you say a man seems to be in good health?"

"You do have really remarkable smiles, Kitty," he murmured.

"It was *ordinary*," she insisted. "But he paused and gave me sort of a look that made me think my hair was falling down. And I had this dreadful fear. But he didn't say anything, just asked me to pour the tea. But now I see he said something to *you*. What did he say?"

He hesitated.

Kitty suffered in silence.

"I think," John said, "it's going to have to be between him and me, for now."

She was still sitting on the floor. She scrambled back onto the chair and wrapped her arms around herself as if chilled.

"What do you mean, between him and you? Either he forbade you from—" she searched for the right word "—from having anything to do with me; or he didn't."

"He trusts my judgment," John said quietly.

"Well," Kitty said as if words were being jerked out of her, "what a cruel friend he is."

He laughed.

What a good day it had been, when he'd first been able to laugh without a stab of pain!

"I don't trust my judgment, I think," he said, no longer laughing, just looking at her; "I'll have to trust yours."

"Oh, no, don't," she begged, trying to smile and make it a joke.

"Get cosy, Kitty, I'm going to tell you a story."

CHAPTER FOURTEEN

SHE TOOK HIM SERIOUSLY. She fetched a spare blanket from the chair John Quire usually used, wrapped it around herself and settled back into the chair by the bed.

John looked across at her from his nest of pillows with a little smile. "Are you nineteen now?"

"Twenty in June."

"I've got seven years on you."

"Thank goodness," said Kitty mildly. "Men are idiots at twenty."

He grinned.

"When I was twenty, I thought I was going to be a draper. I can't say I was *keen* on it, in the way that my father is keen on a fine bolt of bombazine, but it was all right. There was a pretty girl I met at a dance, respectable local tradesman's family. Maria Swann. We got married. My dad helped us set up house. And it wasn't perfect, because life isn't, but we were good together. We were happy to start a family. I put my ear on her belly every day. It was going to be Cora if it was a girl or Jack for a boy.

"And Cora came, and Maria died."

Kitty scrunched down so her face was partly hidden by the blanket. He could see her eyes above it, though, blinking hard.

"And my sister took Cora to nurse, but I didn't know what to do with myself. I wandered around the house bumping into things.

"The funny thing is, it was Maria who made me promise her I'd get out of Leicester. Do something different.

"When I joined the Army I should have just taken the king's shilling like any man. But my family feared for my life; they had money enough; they bought me a commission. The opening for an Ensign got me sent to Portugal with Beresford.

"And there I was—an officer but beneath the others, for I wasn't a gentleman. I'd had as good an education as a well-to-do draper's son could have. Could even talk pretty well. It wasn't enough.

"I didn't let on that I even noticed when they wouldn't include me in a conversation or offer me a drink. It was death by a thousand tiny cuts."

He fell silent. After a moment Kitty prompted: "But Ned...?" sounding hopeful.

John scoffed. "But Ned, nothing! Well, he wasn't the worst of the lot. He treated me just the same as he treated everyone else, which was to say he ignored me.

"There was a time when being ignored was better than being looked down on. Not an Oxford man or a Cambridge one; not a White's man, or Brook's, or Boodle's.

"It sounds like nothing, but when you're a thousand miles from England and there's a few dozen people you're in close quarters with, and they talk and drink with each other, but they all turn their shoulders to you, it matters a lot.

"I did what you do, Kitty; I put on a good face. I was in, and I couldn't face letting them chase me out. I did my duty, made up to the local girls, and pretended it didn't bother me.

"Can you imagine that, Kitty? You can't wonder how I sympathize with Louisa. She made a mistake and fell; I made a mistake by trying to rise.

"And I got the news from my sister that my daughter had died. I hadn't seen her since she was a baby. Never have I felt so much regret in my life, Kitty. I had failed as an officer and as a father. I was going to blow my brains out.

"And Ned came upon me and he gave me this sort of annoyed look and said, 'Oh, forget them! You're a better officer than they'll ever be.'

"I said, 'Them, who cares about them! They can all go hang!' and I told him what had really happened.

"And he just frowned, and said, 'Ah,' and he took my gun away and unloaded it, and then started rummaging through my things and took away my other gun and knife.

"He said, 'I'll tell them you have the fever. You've got a week. I'll send someone with water. Don't disappoint me.'"

Kitty lowered the blanket to smile at him with obvious difficulty. "*That* sounds like Ned."

"He came and sat with me every evening. And it wasn't as if we were bosom friends from then on—but we were brothers.

"*He* wasn't the one to ease my way with our fellow officers, but we could be companions on the outskirts.

"And in 1811 he was wounded, as was I; but I healed and he didn't. He asked me if I would consider selling my commission, and come to Gatewood to be his steward.

"So if you think staying with him as a service I'm doing him, it's not like that. He saved my life, and later on at Albuera I saved his, and he saved my dignity by giving me a respectable way out. War, as I entered it, was a gentleman's game. But I'm no gentleman and there was no way I could play."

She didn't say anything at once. And he was glad, for if she'd said something in haste, especially *I don't care, it doesn't matter*, he would have had to stop her. It did matter.

Finally she said: "I'm so sorry about everything. I'm glad you've found a life here."

"As am I."

"I need to...I need to...." She shook her head. "I came to tell you something. I've had a letter from my sister."

"Which one?"

She blinked. "Susannah, back in London. Her husband, Matthew Sinclaire...he's dying."

"No offence to your brother-in-law, but hasn't he been dying for a long time? He's not very efficient about it. Every time I'm dying, I aim to get it over with quickly, one way or another."

She looked rueful. John knew from Ned that everyone in the

family had pretty much the same sentiment about Matthew Sinclaire.

No hypocrite, Kitty just said judiciously: "You can hardly hold it against a man, that he doesn't die quickly enough."

"People do it all the time," observed John, "especially when he's rich."

"Well he's—" Kitty sighed. "Hush. This is serious. He really *is* dying this time."

"Have you ordered black gloves?" he said pointedly.

"Oh dear." She looked startled, as if necessity of wearing mourning had slipped her mind. "No, but I will."

"Forgive me, I'm going to keep being cynical. You should bear in mind that Ned rolls his eyes every time Mr Sinclaire's name is mentioned."

"That's all very well. But he *is* dying. And I want to be there for my sister."

Oh, so that's what it was. She was leaving.

He pressed his lips together, and didn't answer at once. "So you're off to London, then."

"Soon," said Kitty unhappily, "but I'll come back."

He searched carefully for something to say that didn't make it sound as if he didn't *want* her to come back.

"I think that might be difficult thing for you to manage," he said at last. "If you're under the care of Mrs Whalen, it seems to me she might not care for it if you return—and then go off again straight away."

"Yes, I thought of that. But I—I'll be leaving Miss Green here; I'll have to come back to see her settled somewhere safely."

"You had better see what your brother has to say about that," he said softly.

"I can manage him," said Kitty with confidence. "And I'm going to steal one of the footman as an escort. So I'll have to return *him*."

John laughed despite himself. "Kitty!"

"Not to mention, I want to find out what happened to Will. He didn't answer my last two letters. Susannah said he went to Edinburgh but she didn't say *why*, which isn't like her at all. I want to settle it."

"How long do you intend to be gone?"

"I'm not sure—a fortnight. Not above three weeks."

He forced a smile. She wasn't going to come back. She was going to be swept up in the London scene and her head would be turned by some handsome gentleman. And when the season ended Mrs Whalen would suggest going to Bath or Brighton and how could a young lady resist.

"Well, I may be up and about when you return."

"Oh, that would be so good!"

She flashed a bright smile at him, but it went away again in the next second.

"May I give you that kiss again?" she asked, as if afraid he'd say no. "Since I will miss some."

His good sense—it was about a heaping tablespoon's worth—said No; the rest of him said *Come here; I want you; I want you to have a reason to come back to me*. It was that part which had control over his face.

She came and put her hand on that spot on the bed that by now had a dent in it. He closed his eyes and felt her lips on his. This might be the last time he'd kiss her. It might be the *only* time he'd kiss her like this. He slid his tongue against hers and felt her startled gasp. Then she let him in. Her right hand crept behind his neck, tangling in his hair. Her left hand, from fixing herself in place, was starting to tremble; he could feel it through the bed.

It wasn't true that you only live once. He was, perhaps, on his fourth or fifth life. This one was *The life where I'm in love with Kitty Fairwell* and he didn't know how much longer it would last, but he didn't want to look back and wonder what it was like to touch her.

He ran his single free hand from her shoulder down her bare arm and up again. He couldn't pull her down with him, but he could invite. She was so slender and delicate—sometimes he forgot, because her spirit seemed bigger—he probably *could* pull her onto the bed with one hand. But no, if she was going to end up on the bed, she had to do it herself.

The temptation grew harder to resist. He pushed his hand into her hair, digging his fingers between thick curls. She moaned against his mouth and then crawled onto the bed with him. Oh God yes. There were still these pillows between them, but he'd give it a minute before—and before he could finish the thought she'd tossed one to the floor and kicked the other one out of the way. He guessed he shouldn't be surprised she knew what she wanted. She pressed her whole length against him and he heard himself make a sound. She had the idea of tongues now and she was teasing him with hers.

He knew what he wasn't going to do—even though he wanted to so much—but how much was too much? Could he run his hand along her back, span the bend of her waist with his fingers, cup her buttock with his palm? Pull her toward him until her belly pressed up against his cock, separated from him by only a thin muslin dress and a sheet? He rubbed against her with the agonizing pleasure of it, then made himself stop. The pulling pain in his back wasn't the only reason; he needed to slow down. He wanted to make her whimper and shake under his hand. Then and only then could he ask her to try her hands or her mouth.

He pushed her onto her back with his hand on her shoulder, and leaning toward her as much as he dared, he tugged down the bodice of her dress. A little more manoeuvring, some wiggling on her part, and her breasts were freed from her stays. He spanned one approvingly with his hand, but was frustrated by the way his right arm was still wedged fast by pillows.

"Move up a little," he murmured. "Those want kissing."

"Oh." She wiggled up. He took a nipple in his mouth and tested her with his teeth. "*Ohh!*"

He laughed and just kissed. He looked up at her. By God she was beautiful. Her hair had come down as it did at the slightest opportunity. It sprawled across her shoulders, chestnut with each curl shot through with gold. She was grinning.

"Hullo, Katherine Fairwell."

"Why Katherine?" she asked lazily.

"Because it's a woman's name. And you seem to be very much a woman. Kitty's good, if you're going in disguise as a young lady."

"I see your point."

He grinned. "Do you? Thought I was still wearing a sheet."

She rolled her eyes, flushing. "Ha, ha."

"Come down here, your hair is driving me mad."

"Better than breasts?" she wanted to know. She scooted down and flicked it across his face teasingly.

He buried his face in it like he'd so often imagined. He couldn't take it any more. He slid his hand under the skirt of her dress, squeezed a bare buttock, and ran a finger lightly between her legs. She gasped. She was wet already. It was going to be hard not to dip into her too far, but—well, he was just going to have to marry her, wasn't he; he could wait. He rubbed his thumb against her.

She went tense. "No—stop!"

He stilled his hand but didn't pull his face out of her curls. "I'm not going to get you in trouble, Kitty, I swear. Plenty of good things to do that don't risk that."

"I—it's not that. There is, ah, I have—When I was in London I had an agreement with a gentleman."

He drew back and stared at her blankly. "What?"

"Percy Wolcott. Just before I left London."

"You had an *agreement*? You were engaged? You *are* engaged?"

"We agreed. He was going to write to my father."

"Was going to? Did?"

"Yes. My father won't approve until he meets him, but—there's no reason why he won't."

"Right. Right. Who else knew about this?"

"His family. Susannah. Mrs Whalen. It was the day I was going to tell everyone when Louisa needed help."

"Ned didn't know?"

"No, of course not!"

"Why the hell 'of course not,' Kitty! If you're in love with this man and you want to marry him, you should be so damn excited you want to hang off the church steeple and shout it!"

She seemed to be at a complete loss. "He's just very nice," she stammered.

"Oh, get out."

"If you want me to get out you've got to let go of me."

He realized that he still had his arm tight around her. "No," he said in agony. He made himself let go, feeling instantly cold. "Go. Get out and go to London."

She had to pause to right her clothing. He kept his eyes squeezed shut until he heard the soft sound of the door opening and closing.

How could you, how could you, how could you, he thought after her.

But at the same time, he was thinking: well, she never lied to you, did she. And she doesn't want to marry this Mr Wolcott, whoever he is. But she's right, she should marry him and not me.

He wouldn't think about Kitty Fairwell anymore. He wouldn't dream about her. Except for this one last time, when he'd go past what he'd permitted himself to think. He took himself in hand and imagined the sweet feel of being inside Kitty—Katherine Fairwell. The way she'd smile up at him and gasp as he started to move. He didn't even remember the last time he'd been inside a woman.

He spent abruptly on the sheet and then felt like a sad fool.

CHAPTER FIFTEEN

KITTY WAS UNBEARABLY ashamed. She couldn't *regret* what had happened; when she thought of it, she shivered with the glory of new knowledge. Indeed, she wished it had gone a great deal further. *That* was not the issue.

It was that she had—not to put too fine a point on it— forgotten about Percy Wolcott, and for that, she disliked herself in quite strong terms. Which terms directed towards herself every time she looked in a mirror. Thank *goodness* she'd stopped as soon as she'd remembered.

She needed to—perhaps—either—well, she needed to talk to Percy, *that* was for certain. More than that she couldn't commit to— even in her own head.

It was good that she was going to London to see Susannah, because then she wouldn't have to explain an abrupt departure to Ned. If she'd been more designing or more honest, she would have made speaking to Percy her superior, rather than her secondary reason, but it hadn't seemed so…urgent. Until this morning.

Since Ned had been staying at night with John, and sleeping midmorning through the afternoon, he had become accustomed to eating dinner with John in the Italian room, as *his* breakfast. Still, there was a brief interim period—after dressing, before dinner, whilst drinking tea and reading the post—in which Kitty could catch him.

In the library, naturally. After some weeks of hiding Miss Horne had eventually claimed the saloon—"the best light for needlework," she said defensively—and Ned wasn't using it; so Kitty had given in and let her.

She would never again be friendly to Miss Horne. No repentance; no forgiveness. But she had resumed tolerating her, feeling she had no other choice if she wanted to see Louisa. (Neither of the two young women was fond of needlework, and Jane had filched *Pride and Prejudice* and it was making the rounds of the servants, so Kitty was reading aloud an old favourite by Mrs Radcliffe.)

Today Kitty knocked on the door to the library glad to have a task she was sure of. There were other things she had made a right mess of. Sorting out the details of a trip to London with Ned was positively relaxing by comparison.

"Come in."

"Good day, Ned."

Ned was sitting at the table by the window to read the post. He adjusted his head to look at her with his good eye. "Kitty."

That brief acknowledgment was a small step away from saying "What do you want?" A *small* step, but still, a step.

"Did you also get a letter from Susannah?"

"Yes. You should go visit her."

Kitty raised her eyebrows. That was useful. "I quite agree. That's why I'm here."

He jerked sharply as if he hadn't imagined that would work. He stared at her, looking lost rather than pleased.

"May I join you?" she prompted.

"Go ahead and sit, but I've only got one—" he gestured at the setting on his breakfast tray.

She sat across from him and leaned into the sun coming through the window. "I'm all right, thank you. I'm going to see Susannah; tomorrow, if you can spare the carriage. I will be back in two or three weeks."

"Why? I mean, why are you coming back…." Even whilst he was in the middle of saying it he looked as if he regretted asking.

She smiled at him. "Because I adore your company."

"Very funny."

"I wasn't joking; it's true. But, primarily, I will be returning to take Louisa and Miss Horne."

Ned stared at her. "No, you certainly aren't! Take those damned women with you *now*."

"I will—when I come back; but I can't very well take them to Susannah's."

"Deal with them first, and *then* go, and—" He lost the end of the sentence abruptly, and looked embarrassed. Kitty wondered if he'd really been about to say "and don't come back." But he hadn't, and it filled her up with happiness.

She stood and went around the table and kissed him on the thinning patch in his black hair. He held quite still whilst she did it but when she settled down again, he said, with the gruffness she was by now quite immune to: "Don't try to charm me, Kitty."

"Whilst I'm in London, I'll be making inquiries about a cottage for them. If you wanted to help, you could write to any acquaintance you might think of." She sighed, looking out at the sunny front lawn with the drive arcing through it. "It's just such a pity Gatewood hasn't a dower house—what an easy solution that would be!"

"Thank God it hasn't! My reputation is bad enough; I don't need to be known for keeping a fallen woman within arm's reach. And you can bet within two months everyone would say *I* was the one who ruined her. I don't have much pride, but I'd prefer to be judged only for sins I'm guilty of, if you please."

"All right," Kitty said hastily. She hadn't thought of that. "I beg your pardon. But we haven't a dower house in any event."

"No. Instead, you intend to leave her in my *actual* house."

"Chaperoned," said Kitty, hearing the word as flimsy even as she said it.

"Oh, yes, because Miss Horne has done such a brilliant work of *that*."

Kitty had no argument there, and left it alone. "Well, it's for two or three weeks; and it's not as if you have callers who will spread rumours. And if the *servants* talk—they'll say that you detest her."

Ned wrinkled his nose.

"Besides, it will give you quite the encouragement to seek out a place for her." She had a sudden thought. Arranging everything had so many ins and outs to keep track of! "*Not*, of course, that you ought to send her off without letting me investigate if it's a suitable arrangement or not. Ladies have to take more things into account than gentlemen. But you see what you can find; and so will I; and as soon as I come back we will see which seems best."

"I dare say Miss Horne will reject them all for trifling reasons. The room and board she is currently squeezing out of Fairwell pockets is much better than whatever the two of them will manage on 20*l.* a year." He gave her a level look. "Or that, plus whatever *you* were going to give them."

Kitty didn't do him the disservice of denying it. "*I* dare say they need it more than my *modiste*."

He didn't argue. He just said, "Will has rubbed off on you."

"Well, if half the people in the world make fun of us for being misers, and the other half for our being excessively charitable—*that* is a reputation I can stomach."

He said, "Hmph." And then, after drinking some tea: "But I still don't give you permission to leave Miss Green and her insufferable companion. I don't like either of them. You'll take them with you."

"*Ned!*" Kitty squalled. "Hasn't Louisa been helpful in watching over John?"

"Thomas can do it. Lord knows, he's not good at cleaning boots."

She decided it was a bad moment to mention that she was borrowing Adam, so Ned was going to be a footman down. Adam and Jane were sweet on each other; Kitty was hopeless to resist giving them such a good opportunity.

"You have an entire manor to yourself! You needn't see them if you don't wish to."

"But I'll know they're here," he said implacably, "and so will everyone else. It wouldn't be doing them any favours."

Kitty took a deep breath.

"Very well. I will take them with me. I'll put them up in a hotel until I find a place for them. Since you have not a chivalrous bone in your body."

"Good."

"*Except* that one time when you were home from school and a bull chased me up a tree and I twisted my ankle getting down and you carried me all the way home. It was *miles*."

He glared at her. "You were ten years old, Kitty, what was I going to do? Leave you under the hedge and hope the bull didn't come back?"

"And then when you and Robert told Matthew Sinclaire what you'd do to him if he didn't treat Susannah well. I believe your promise was that you'd remove his teeth. One. By. One."

Ned went suddenly pale. "You overheard that? Kitty, by God, you never told anyone, did you?"

"Of course not. Even at age six, I realized you could get in trouble for threatening your future brother-in-law with traumatic dental work."

He was staring at her in horror. "Did you even know what we were talking about?"

"Not really. But I was fascinated by the idea of taking out someone's teeth as punishment. I spent a while wondering whether you'd start with the front, since they'd be easier to get to, or the back, so it didn't spoil his looks so quickly."

Ned looked satisfyingly taken down a peg. Several pegs.

"And there was that moment when you ripped up Bastable and Louisa's marriage license, cool as you please," said Kitty as a finishing shot. "*That* was chivalrous. Also dramatic. Did I tell you how proud I was of you? I don't believe I did."

He frowned; then sighed, and put up his eyes toward the ceiling. "All right. *Very well*. You win, Kitty. For the next three weeks, *no longer*, this will be Ned Fairwell's Home for Wayward Girls. Just tell them to keep out of my way. And come back and deal with them soon. *Please*."

"Of course! I don't want your reputation to suffer."

*

Kitty felt rather grand rattling into London in a carriage with Fair-well arms on the door. She wasn't a Lady Anything but there was a lot to be said for money and malleable brothers. For the moment she had somehow secured the dispensation of her own business.

Whilst she knew it would be more polite to settle in at Mrs Whalen's and then call on Susannah, she was feeling less than enthusiastic about the prospect of meeting Mrs Whalen. There would be scoldings, and she would be expected to bow her head and apologize meekly. She was not in the mood. At the moment the reason for making up to Mrs Whalen escaped her.

She had the carriage stop in Mayfair in front of Forester House, which was ostensibly the home of her brother-in-law Mr Sinclaire—assuming he hadn't died, of course—but was actually on indefinite loan from the Fairwell estate for as long as Susannah cared to use it.

Forester House was a terrace house in red brick with white windows, four stories tall, with a black railing around the front to keep one from falling to the kitchen level and tradesman's entrance below-ground.

The house adjoining on one side was white stone, and the house on the other side was brick with marble columns on either side of the door; but other than small variations in finish and decoration, one house could scarcely be told from another. Susannah was not the kind of woman who would add columns where no columns had been provided, so the house was simple.

Adam hopped down from the carriage and rapped on the door. Kitty could hear the butler starting to tell him that the Sinclaires were not accepting visitors (which answered Kitty's question of whether the Sinclaires were still plural, or singular). Then the butler must have identified the carriage, as his tone changed from denial to surprise.

Very shortly Kitty was inside.

"Will you be staying with us, Miss?" asked the butler, whose

name, inevitably, was John, though he was called by his surname of
Bunting.

"We'll see," said Kitty, "if you would please go inquire of my
sister whether she would like company, or if she would consider a
houseguest burdensome."

From the lonely tone of her last letter Kitty suspected it may
well be the former.

The butler vanished upstairs. Kitty waited, unwilling even to
take her bonnet off or have her luggage (such as it was) brought in.

She heard a quick step coming down the stairs and her older
sister pounced on her, squashing her bonnet and squeezing her so
that Kitty could hardly breathe. Her embrace had something of
desperation about it, as if Susannah didn't want to let go. "Of course
you should stay! Bunting, please have my sister's things brought in."

Kitty left Adam to see to the carriage, and followed Susannah
upstairs into the drawing-room on the first floor.

Usually, Susannah was a quiet woman with a sort of thoughtful
solemnity Kitty admired but couldn't even pretend to mimic.
Possibly, Kitty thought privately, it had something to do with having
been married to a dying man for a long time. A certain amount of
decorum seemed proper.

Susannah sank down into a chair by the window that looked out
over the garden and the mews.

She was thirty years old and strikingly beautiful, in a warm,
feminine way, unlike her handsome full sister Julia who always had
the look of someone putting on an act. Susannah's most striking
feature were giant, mesmerizing blue-grey eyes, though as usual the
skin under them was dark with want of sleep.

Like both Julia and Ned, she had very dark hair, a tall, full
figure, and slightly olive skin. Impolite people remarked on this
when any of the older three were standing next to pale, slight Kitty,
Will, or Henry. One could, of course, simply ignore impolite
comments. They all did so assiduously.

"I'm so glad you're here." Susannah always had a soft but clear voice. She had composed herself from her enthusiasm of a moment ago, but still she leaned forward slightly as if to absorb Kitty's warmth. "Can you stay long?"

In retrospect Kitty's promise of "two or three weeks" seemed rash.

"I was thinking two or three weeks—I still have things to do at Gatewood House—but I can stay longer if you need me."

Susannah cocked her head. "What do you have still to do at Gatewood? Does it have to do with Miss Green?"

"Yes; I'm going to find her and Miss Horne a cottage safe somewhere, and I'd like to make sure they have everything they need."

"That's good of you, Kitty."

Susannah was the last woman in the world who was going to judge a woman for having relations with a man before marriage. In her case, she'd ended up with Eliza. Kitty wondered briefly how her life might have gone if she *hadn't* ended up with Eliza.

"How is—" Kitty waved her hand ineffectually. "It seems so rude to ask."

"He can't breathe any more," said Susannah in a low but frank voice. "Mr Rees says he believes the growth has spread to his lungs."

"Mr Rees is—"

"The surgeon-apothecary."

"Don't you have a physician?"

"Mr Sinclaire objects to being bled and Mr Rees was the only medical man he could find who wouldn't argue. And didn't try to give him what Mr Sinclaire calls 'witch's brews.'"

Kitty thought to herself that if she were an apothecary and she had a client who was willing to pay to not receive any treatment, she might consider that an excellent business.

She said only: "Ned is of the same opinion; he wouldn't hear of having John—Stanger bled after he was shot. And he seems to be healing well, so I suppose it was all right."

"You know, the first physician we had in gave Mr Sinclaire two months to live?" said Susannah in a detached voice. "Mr Sinclaire said if he had two months to live he didn't want to spend it being chopped up. I remonstrated with him, but now it's six years later."

"How—how are *you* feeling?" asked Kitty tentatively, peering at her sister's large, haunted eyes.

Susannah looked back at the door to make sure it was closed. "Exhausted," she murmured. "Sad. Hopeful." Then with cold, hard vehemence: "I regret that I won't wake up one day and find my name has transformed back to 'Susannah Fairwell.'"

"Oh," Kitty said, feeling inadequate.

"Are you surprised?"

Kitty hesitated. "No. But—I'm sorry; that's all. Did you ever love him?"

"Oh yes. For a while." Susannah's voice was low and flat again. "You should have seen him when he was healthy. He had the finest legs and the most striking red hair. But I should never have married him."

"Did he mistreat you?" said Kitty tremulously.

"No." She shook her head slowly. "But he didn't *like* me. And I didn't like him. Before he got ill we used to scream at each other. About everything, from the time dinner was served to what sort of boots I'd bought. He was impossibly childish and could never just— let anything be." She took a breath. "And he would say the same thing about me. I don't *want* to be difficult, but I could never seem to just go along. I wish I'd—I wish I'd let him see how I was, before we married. When we were young and I wanted him, I tried to be agreeable, to show only my good side. Once he knew me for who I am, he thought me a shrew."

"What a fool he was!" said Kitty softly. "He should have adored you. You're perfect."

Susannah was startled into a laugh. "Oh, Kitty, you are the best sister anyone could ask for."

"I've been trying to distribute a little," said Kitty, "and be a better sister to Ned. He's such a—a—an unforgivable something; but he's so sweet; if he loves you he'd walk through fire for you."

"An 'unforgivable something'?" Susannah put her eyes up to the ceiling. "And *I* am 'perfect.' You *do* see the best in people, Kitty."

"Well, why not."

Someone knocked on the door. Susannah said, "Come in."

Bunting stuck in his head. "Mr Rees to see Mr Sinclaire, ma'am."

"Please take him up." Susannah hesitated. "And send him in here when he's done."

Bunting's frown was haughty. "Yes, ma'am."

When he was gone, Susannah said, "So now you know. Will you forgive me?"

"There's nothing to forgive!" Kitty scrambled forward and gave her a kiss.

Susannah wiped her eyes on her sleeve. "Now that you're here, you can distract me. I have something to settle with you. Are you, or are you not, engaged to Percy Wolcott?"

Kitty sat, and blushed fiercely.

"Well?" demanded Susannah. "It has a yes or no answer."

"He wrote to Papa but Papa won't agree before meeting him."

Susannah pressed her lips together. "Mr Wolcott seems like a gentlemanly young man. And he clearly adores you."

Kitty thought it perfectly possible that they had met at one of the small social functions Susannah permitted herself. But Percy hadn't made any public scene of his affection. "How do you—?"

"He called. He begged that I might be able to make the situation move along faster. Then, realizing Mr Sinclaire was dying, he begged my pardon and left. Which speaks well for the nicety of his manners, I suppose."

"Yes," Kitty said in a small voice, "his manners are invariably nice. And he does adore me."

Susannah gave her a fierce, daggering stare that made Kitty squeak as if it had actually scraped her skin. "And what *else* do you think about Percy Wolcott, Miss Katherine Fairwell?" Susannah said dangerously.

"I have absolutely no complaints about him. He is agreeable in every way. Not," Kitty hastened to add, "so agreeable that I feel he is just trying to make up to me. We disagreed extensively on whether fox-hunting is cruel; and on whether music or the theatre is better; and whether it would be right to receive Bonaparte at dinner; and all sorts of things like that. And I don't have a complaint about the way he argues."

"And yet," Susannah said.

Kitty said baldly, "Well, we were in the garden at Lady Dearman's party and we kissed quite a bit and it was pleasant. Up until that point, pleasant seemed like enough. I'm not certain it is any more."

Susannah gave her a hard look. "What made you change your mind?"

Kitty hadn't decided yet how much to say. She started somewhere, feeling bravery was necessary. "Talking to Miss Green." She gulped. "Miss Green, to be frank, is familiar with the concept of lust. And it doesn't seem to be what I feel for Percy, or the reverse. But it d-doesn't seem to be a good idea to be led by—that. It didn't bring you or Louisa any joy. So perhaps I ought to marry Percy Wolcott. It seems as if we thoroughly suit."

"Or you might discover you don't suit at all," said Susannah, low and cynical, "and you won't even have the pleasure of your bed to make up for it."

"You might as well say I shouldn't marry at all, because it *might* go wrong," said Kitty with some warmth, "but I do want to; I want to have a family and my own house; I know there will always be *some* difficulties but I would rather face them honestly than be an old maid."

Susannah said, "Excuse me." She rose, and walked around the room, her long pale grey dress swaying around her. Kitty remembered that Ned used to do this too, before he was hurt; he would move around running into things and getting irritated that they were in his way. Susannah paced.

"I agree with Miss Green," she said finally. "Kisses ought to be more than *pleasant*. You ought not marry a man who doesn't stir you.

"But you're right, a marriage is built on more than lust. Marry in haste—repent at leisure. There must be an equality of minds, also. A meeting of character. I never had that with Matthew."

"What if I never meet a man with whom I can meet both body and soul?"

Susannah sank back into her chair. "We're lucky; we don't have to marry for money."

Kitty looked at her. "You don't seem lucky," she said carefully.

"I feel lucky." Susannah was crying, great round drops rolling down her face. "It's slow and sometimes evil luck. But I love my girls. And soon I'll be free."

CHAPTER SIXTEEN

SOMEONE KNOCKED ON THE door again. Susannah wiped her face hastily. "Do I look all right?"

Kitty wasn't going to lie to her. "You look like a woman whose husband is dying," she said gently.

Susannah grimaced, gave her face another wipe, and turned to look toward the door.

The surgeon-apothecary in his blood-stained leather apron stopped just inside the room. He was a tall angular man with cutting cheekbones and close-cropped curly dark hair. He gave Susannah a peculiar, and Kitty felt, a familiar look.

"I beg your pardon, Mrs Sinclaire." He had a Welsh accent but a short way of speaking. "I didn't realize you had a visitor. I'll go."

"No, it's all right, Mr Rees. This is my sister."

He looked between the two of them and raised a sharp dark eyebrow, rather rudely, Kitty thought. Susannah hastened to add: "My half-sister. Kitty Fairwell."

"Good day, Miss," he said neutrally, with a slight inclination of his head.

Kitty was not sure how one was supposed to act when being half-introduced to one's dying brother-in-law's apothecary. And Susannah had always been the proper one!

Kitty nodded and said, "Good day, Mr Rees," because that seemed to be safe under any circumstance.

"How is Mr Sinclaire—" said Susannah. "You can speak in front of Miss Fairwell."

"Mr Sinclaire's ability to remain living despite all odds is a continual source of astonishment to me." Welsh accents were known to be musical and charming, but he had a rather dry, sarcastic way of speaking. "For another man, I'd say days. For him—" He shrugged. He appeared to think for a second. He added, "I'm sorry." Apparently because he knew he had to.

"Yes, thank you, Mr Rees," said Susannah. "Bunting will see to your fee. Thank you for coming."

It wasn't that Mr Rees looked at Susannah gently; he didn't seem to have any tender expression; it was just the way the corner of his proud mouth angled down as if he really were sorry. "Yes, Mrs Sinclaire. Good day, ma'am. Good day, Miss Fairwell."

He left. After the door was firmly shut, Kitty said doubtfully, "Was he a little rude?"

Turning back to her, Susannah's eyes were wide. "Was he?" she said slowly. "I don't know; he's just like that. He never tried to lie to Mr Sinclaire or me, and say it would be all right. I suppose this is the one thing Mr Sinclaire and I have agreed upon." She smiled faintly.

"Oh, I see," said Kitty, who didn't entirely.

"Isn't it odd to think you've seen someone so often and then things change, and you don't see them again?" said Susannah in a queer voice. "As if your neighbour moves to another city, or your butler takes a different job? It doesn't matter, but it's hard to grasp."

Kitty almost said "*Oh*," out loud, but instead she said it rather loudly inside her own head. Good heavens. Had there actually been something—? No; there had been nothing in the slightest bit suggestive about his look; it was really what Susannah had said: that she didn't expect to see him again.

(Perhaps not *only* that, Kitty thought. On her side.)

"I think you ought to see Mr Wolcott as soon as you can," said Susannah, "and be frank with him. Not, I mean, about what you talked about with Miss Green—but, to be honest, if he's interested in you, then he ought be eager to give you a kiss. Can you get him alone?"

Kitty flushed. "I don't know; it's always his sisters I call on. No, I'm sure I can manage it. He should *want* to be alone with me. You're right. It's too bad you can't chaperon, or I'd suggest he take me on a drive in the Park."

Susannah was leaning forward, looking at her face intently. "But will you really break it off? It can be harder to say no than you think. He might make it sound reasonable. If you don't intend to stick to what you've decided, just go—be happy with your agreeable young man." She sounded strangled, as if she hated herself for saying it. "If you don't know anything different, perhaps you'll soon find it doesn't matter."

Kitty blushed and looked at her teacup.

Susannah sat up straight and her voice became brisk. "I don't want to know who he is. Just don't tell me you made my mistake."

"I haven't."

"But now you know."

"Yes."

"Well, thank goodness," said Susannah, in sort of a relieved angry voice. "Better you find out now, than when you've been married for ten years and suddenly get a *tendre* for one of the footmen."

Kitty raised her eyes. "Or the apothecary?" she dared. She felt, suddenly, absolutely, like a Katherine Fairwell—a grown woman settling affairs of the heart with her sister.

Susannah froze with her teacup in hand. After a second the teacup started to shake. She lowered it carefully. "Was it obvious?"

"No, not at all; except that you tried to tell me. But there's nothing on his side, is there?"

"Men look at me," said Susannah flatly. "Him too. But never—any expression on either side. I trust you not to tell anyone. Not even Will, or your friends, or Percy Wolcott if you marry him."

"I'll take it with me to the grave. You like him very much, don't you."

Susannah said flatly, "If anyone could see what's in my head they'd burn me at the stake."

"I wouldn't," Kitty said.

"Why did he have to be a *surgeon*," said Susannah with gritted teeth. "Not a physician."

"It makes me feel better," said Kitty, "because I've got it for Ned's estate manager."

Susannah looked astonished, and then cackled at the shared absurdity of their situations.

"The trouble is, I think I want to marry him. I mean, I *do* want to marry him."

Susannah stopped laughing.

"We suit each other much better than Percy and I ever could. I *like* balls and fine gowns and French cheese and eavesdropping on scandalous gossip. But I *also* like dealing with chickens and the four-course field rotation and arranging things the way I like them and wearing muddy boots to church. And I want to rip his clothes off."

Susannah was just staring at her. Kitty looked her sister in the eyes.

"It would be a scandal. He was an officer with Ned, but his family are drapers in Leicester and that's how people would describe him. The draper's son. And I don't care on my own account, because I'm all right dealing with chickens. But you've got three daughters and you'll be bringing Eliza out in a few years. And Will should get married, and Henry and Robert if they ever bother, and you'll want to remarry, I suspect. So how bad is it going to be?"

Susannah took a breath. Then another, and another, slowly.

"If you don't want to marry Wolcott then you must get out of it, Kitty," she said in agony. "You must not marry him. Your engagement hasn't been announced yet, after all.

"Whether you marry this other man...I don't know. I don't *know* how bad it would be."

"Would your friends drop you?" Kitty asked softly.

Susannah thought for a while. She closed her eyes briefly.

"I don't have many friends any more. There are still a few kind people who invite me to things. I don't know if I'd even notice if they stopped. Please don't ask me about that."

"I know I'll lose some of mine," Kitty said steadily. "Miss Price has stopped writing back to me because of Louisa. She can't associate with me, she said."

"Oh, Kitty."

"And that would be just the beginning."

Susannah nodded.

Kitty was not going to spare herself anything. "And Eliza will be coming out in a few years."

Susannah's mouth quivered.

Kitty went on. "And Will probably will want to marry some respectable vicar's daughter. If I lost him a chance at happiness I'd never forgive myself."

Susannah's eyes widened. "You don't—? Have you not had a letter from him?"

"No; and he always writes back. Is he not well?"

"He's gone to Edinburgh after an actress. In fact he—he writes that they're engaged; though it's a sham just to help her out."

Kitty nearly fell off her chair. She said something unladylike.

Susannah said, "But men can get away with things we can't. A gentleman after an actress isn't the same as a lady after a tradesman. He'll be forgiven whether it's a sham or not. You wouldn't be."

"I would like Will to get away with something," Kitty said, "for once. But yes. I know."

"I know you do," said Susannah quietly. "Kitty, I can't give you permission. You must make your own choice."

She looked around at the room. "Would he be embarrassed to be here?"

Kitty added an imaginary John Stanger to the drawing-room of the Mayfair house. He leaned on the window-sill and raised his un-brow at her. The light behind him caught the tawny halo of his hair. Being silly, he made a leg, smiling.

"No, he wouldn't. If it was just us." She forced herself to be absolutely truthful. "If Mrs Whalen joined us and tried to terrorize him, he'd get mad at her, I think. But not shouting-mad. He'd—look down his nose at her, I think."

Kitty paused and then continued. "But, you know—so would

Ned, and he'd be rude about it. Robert makes fun of her behind her back. And Will sidles away trying to avoid her. So I'd vouch for *John's* manners over theirs, any day."

"Good manners are not going to be enough for the Mrs Whalens of the world."

"I think I'm trying to see if it's going to be enough for the Fairwells," Kitty said cautiously.

Susannah was just silent, looking sad.

Kitty said, "You might as well say the last thing you're thinking. I want to hear it now."

"Would he even have you?" Susannah said softly.

"I don't know," said Kitty. "He thinks I led him on, which I did because I was being dreadfully stupid, but I'm trying to fix that now. But whether he would want to risk going in with me—despite the Mrs Whalens of the world he'll never be good enough for—I truly don't know. And I'm afraid."

"Me too," said Susannah.

Regrettably, now that Kitty was in London she didn't feel that she could make calls without the chaperonage of a married woman. She knew the Wolcotts *well*, but they were not bosom friends. In this instance, a footman wouldn't do. And Susannah, of course, was occupied.

Therefore, it was necessary to make up to Mrs Whalen.

As soon as Kitty changed out of her traveling dress, she gritted her teeth, put on a smile, and summoned the carriage again.

Despite it being after the hours for morning visits, she was at once admitted to the Whalens'. After all, Kitty had, until recently, lived there.

Mrs Whalen did not make her wait even five minutes before she came tripping downstairs to scold her.

Kitty apologized profusely for any and all inconvenience. Privately, she observed how Mrs Whalen had not indeed been inconvenienced in the slightest. (Unless it was by Will's abrupt remove to Edinburgh. Mrs Whalen wanted him for her ward, Miss Fettinger.)

Kitty was forgiven. She *was* aware that this rapid forgiveness had something do with the way Kitty had suggested going shopping with Miss Fettinger. Kitty—sad as it was to say!—was soon going to need some black gowns with deep hems; but Miss Fettinger could *certainly* get something more cheerful. Kitty *owed* it to Miss Fettinger as an apology for not writing individually to *her* as opposed to just Mrs Whalen.

(Kitty thought this sounded like a plausible excuse. Miss Fettinger was a good-hearted but tedious young woman who would never have expected Kitty to write.)

The fact that Kitty wanted to call on the Wolcotts as soon as possible was also in her favour. The Whalens and the Wolcotts were friends; that was indeed how Kitty had made the acquaintance first of the Misses Wolcott, and then Percy. Mrs Whalen, feeling nervously responsible for the match, was only too eager to have it settled.

That tiresome task accomplished, Kitty went back to Susannah's. She wanted to see her three nieces—thirteen-year-old Eliza with her father's red hair, eleven-year-old Tansy, and seven-year-old Sally.

Kitty wished she could just *know* what would happen. What people would say. The worst thing she could think of was hurting her family.

She was rich enough to get her way with Mrs Whalen; did that mean she was *too* rich to marry a draper's son, and not be muttered about for years to come?

The next day, Kitty looked up at the grand front of the Wolcott home and was still afraid.

"Don't mention Miss Green," warned Mrs Whalen.

"I will not bring her up," said Kitty quietly. "But they might ask."

Mrs Whalen huffed. "I should hardly think it proper conversation."

"Indeed not," said Kitty.

Mrs Whalen eyed her. She kept looking as if she found Kitty inexplicable.

Caroline and Mary Wolcott greeted Kitty with enthusiasm. They, too, seemed to have been warned not to mention Miss Green. Kitty was either relieved or passionately disappointed that Percy was not present (though she saw Mrs Wolcott making an aside to the butler, so she wondered if he might soon appear).

The topic of Kitty and Percy's engagement was also not, it seemed, within Caroline and Mary's approved list of things to broach. Except indirectly.

"Have you heard from your father?" asked Caroline eagerly. She was a bouncing, ringletted brunette rather past her prime.

"Yes; a letter from him awaited me at Mrs Whalen's," said Kitty.

She had read it and it didn't make her decision either easier, or more difficult. How she loved him!

Caroline and Mary—who was a younger, plumper version of her sister—exchanged a meaningful glance.

"Is it possible that Percy...might be traveling soon?" inquired Mary.

"He has been *so* eager to hear from you!" put in Caroline.

"And for my part, I quite look forward to seeing him again!" said Kitty truthfully, smiling at the Wolcott sisters.

They were not foolish enough to fail to understand that Kitty was putting them off. Caroline was tactful and changed the subject.

"How did you find Gatewood House, Miss Fairwell? Is it very grand?"

"No; not for a country house; it is only a villa. And it is a little in need of repair. That was one of the matters I was seeing to whilst I was there."

"But what is it *like*? Has it a good prospect? Are the grounds pleasing? Did you see any society?"

"It's beautiful," said Kitty. "All golden stone, with columns in front." They sighed. Columns! "As for the grounds, the *wood* of the name tells the truth. You can hardly pass beyond the end of the lawn. And for society, no; not unless you count the under-bailiff John Tickle. And the chickens."

She was smiling, and Caroline and Mary quite fairly took it as a joke.

"Time in the country has made your head full of corn, Miss Fairwell," teased Mary.

"Wheat, barley, and turnips," Kitty agreed amiably.

"Barley? Who eats barley?"

"The poor," said Kitty, not sighing, but thinking a sigh in her head; "but mostly one makes beer out of it."

"Does one make beer out of turnips also?" murmured Mary.

"No, sheep and cattle eat them in the winter," said Kitty. Then some little devil made her add: "One *also* undersows with clover and ryegrass, of course, which are good fodder. You get the richest manure with this system."

They glanced at each other, not even shocked so much as bewildered. Kitty smiled at them.

She heard the door, and Percy's jovial voice, and a clomp of his boots. In only a moment he burst in.

"Miss Fairwell, Miss Fairwell!"

He took her hand and kissed it most fervently. Kitty's heart could not help but flutter.

"Mr Wolcott!" she said, laughing, "I am gone for a few weeks and return to discover you've grown a moustache! Is this timing because you feared I wouldn't approve?"

"A few weeks, Miss Fairwell? It felt like an eternity!" He tweaked the end of his glossy black moustache with a worried expression. "But if you don't approve, I'll have it off as quickly as I can summon my valet."

"No, no, it looks exceptionally dashing on you. You are too sweet." Kitty hadn't planned this in advance. She said, "Do let me see how it looks with your hat."

Percy blinked. "My hat?"

"Quite!" said Kitty firmly. She had allowed him to keep his grasp on her hand and she now squeezed his fingers. "Did you leave it in the hall?"

"Go show Miss Fairwell how your moustache looks with your hat, darling," said Mrs Wolcott. She didn't sigh, but she gave the impression.

"And then come back and show us," said Mrs Whalen firmly.

Percy, being a gentleman, was a little bit slower than a lady, but he caught on.

The Wolcotts lived in another tall terrace house; Kitty left the room to the drawing-room open a crack but then led Percy downstairs directly to the front hall. The butler was there.

"A moment, if you please, Sprint," said Percy cheerfully.

Percy put on his stylishly tall top hat. It was as glossy black as his moustache. He posed a little, flexing his broad shoulders. "What do you think, Miss Fairwell?"

"I think you do look really very good, Mr Wolcott," Kitty murmured. Why couldn't anything be easy? She glanced to the side; the butler had gone. "Mr Wolcott, may I kiss you?"

Percy Wolcott looked startled.

"I missed you," said Kitty firmly. This had occasionally been true.

"Oh dear girl!" said Percy fondly. He swooped down and gave her a peck. She felt his moustache more than his lips. Then he was gone again.

Kitty sighed inside. She stood on tiptoe and planted one hand on each of Percy's shoulders. "Mr Wolcott, do look me in the eye for a moment. Thank you."

He frowned, peering down at her with concern. "Are you quite all right, Miss Fairwell? I missed you awfully, too, you know! I'm sorry about that business with Bastable and your friend. Fancy him turning out to be such an arse!"

"You are lovely, Percy," said Kitty, exasperated. "You don't happen to stay awake thinking of wedding nights, do you?"

He looked at her uncomprehending; then blushed.

"That blush is a good sign," murmured Kitty. Then: "Do you ever feel that we suit in all possible ways except that we don't keep each other up at night?"

He lowered his voice to a whisper. "What's this about?"

"You know perfectly well; if you're going to plead ignorance then you're a fool."

He chewed on the thought. "It just—*that* isn't everything, Miss Fairwell. Are you going to let that spoil it? Don't you think it'll come in time?"

"I very much wish I wasn't going to let that spoil it, Percy."

His face fell. His eyes searched her expression sadly. "Miss Green didn't put any ideas into your head, did she?"

"This problem had already occurred to me, I'm afraid."

He tipped forward and gave her another little kiss. Kitty appreciated that he was trying. She did her best, for the sake of giving him a fair chance.

She took her hands off his shoulders. "I believe I ought to go now," she said sadly. She turned and started up the stair to fetch Mrs Whalen and give her truly heartfelt regrets to the Wolcotts.

"Is it the moustache?" Percy called after her.

Kitty turned back on the stairs and sized him up fondly through watering eyes. "No, Mr Wolcott; the moustache is really quite darling. You ought to keep it. Unless of course you find some lady or gentleman—" he was just slow enough on the uptake that she knew she'd get away with that "—who keeps you up at night, and they don't care for it. There's no accounting for taste."

It turned out to be quite easy to cry when she returned to Susannah's and discovered her brother-in-law had died.

CHAPTER SEVENTEEN

"I'M THINKING ABOUT marrying," said John the day after Kitty left.

He was on his stomach on his bed, sweating. Until a moment ago he'd been stretching his back, just to point of pain. He'd pushed too far by accident, and was regretting it.

Ned was in his customary chair beside him, with his hand resting on the top of his cane. John had kept him company so many times when he was in pain; now he silently repaid the favour.

"Who?" Ned asked quietly.

"Some sensible girl," John said, in agony. "From Glenchester, may be."

"I see."

"I want a family. Not that you're not my brother, but…you're often thoroughly unpleasant."

John slid his eyes over. Ned smiled silently at him.

"The thing is," John said, "I worry about you. If I'm not here. When it gets bad at night. I don't want to desert you."

Ned tipped his head back and looked at the ceiling. He frowned.

"Do you *know* there are cobwebs on your ceiling?" he said.

"If you weren't a lazy arse, you could've hired another maid. And then there would not be cobwebs on my ceiling."

There was a short silence from Ned. "I'll wait for Kitty to come back. She seemed eager to do it and it seems wrong of me to spoil her fun. Am I wrong?"

John pressed his face into the bed. "I'd like to hope you're right. But it seems as if she's got bigger and better things on her mind."

Ned made a little hiss of air through his teeth. That was the sum total of his response until several minutes later.

John occupied himself with trying to remember what article in the Encyclopædia was next waiting for them, as a distraction from several agonies.

"You're not quitting as my estate manager, are you?" said Ned finally.

"Of course not!"

"So bring your wife here, if you like. You can have the whole upstairs as a wedding present. *I'm* not getting married. And I can't get up all the damn stairs."

John thought: I can't imagine someone like Molly Weaver or Sadie Jones living here.

"But, one thing," said Ned pleadingly. "Wait until Miss Green and Miss Horne go? I can be alone. Just not alone with *them*. Miss Horne has shark teeth."

John laughed at him. "Not going anywhere til I can raise my arm without crying like a baby."

After a few days John dared lurch a loop inside the house trying to get his strength back; his legs felt shaky from too much lying down.

"And you're coming with me," he said to Ned; "I've been remiss in chasing you around. How long has it been since you saw the south side of the house?"

Ned grunted. "It's not my fault. It's haunted by a maiden aunt. Even worse. A *poor* maiden aunt."

This turned out to be the case, but Ned had barely time to glare once at Miss Horne before they were rescued by the sound of the footman coming in with the post. John raised his eyebrows at Ned. "Race you."

Ned said something unprintable. Then he won so easily that he stopped and waited for John to catch up.

Two letters for Ned; one with a black border. Ned cracked it open standing in the hall.

"Good riddance," he said succinctly.

John was trying to look as if he weren't wishing one of the letters was for him. One of the non-black-bordered ones, obviously.

"Matthew Sinclaire?" he inquired.

"One and the same. I believe Sooze is actually rather upset. There's no accounting for women."

The other letter Ned looked at without comment and stuck under his arm.

The third letter he passed back to the footman. "This one's for Miss Green."

Since John was no longer helplessly stuck in bed, Ned had moved back to his couch in the library and was sleeping at night again. Or ostensibly sleeping. John felt safe in knocking in the evening.

"Come in."

John stuck his head in through the door. "It's damn cold in my room since you moved back. The maids think *I* deserve only normal amounts of coal."

As he'd expected, Ned was on his couch in the corner facing the fire. Ned stuck his hand over the back of it and flapped it in a "Well, come on," gesture.

John made his way down the wall, mindful of both shaky legs and the stabbing back pain that occurred every time he made the mistake of moving his arm.

John collapsed into the soft chair in the corner with a grunt. "Well met, fellow invalid."

"I've had a letter from Kitty," said Ned.

John didn't know whether he should panic or be over the moon. "You ought to work up to that sort of thing, you know?"

"Oh, you *know* I got one," growled Ned with his usual charm.

"*Yes*, but I didn't expect that you were going to tell me about it —much less start a conversation with it."

"I'm going to read it to you," said Ned.

Ned had often read him particularly entertaining excerpts or important news from his family's letters; it was an ordinary thing to do. In this case, however, John said quickly:

"Don't you think she'd mind?"

"I've read it already, and I think she assumed I would."

A bold and ridiculous hope blossomed in John's chest.

Ned adjusted himself toward the fire, holding the letter at angle where the light fell on it.

John immediately started to grin at Kitty's words in Ned's voice. Perhaps unconsciously, Ned was picking up a hint of her intonation.

> Dear Ned,
>
> By now you've received the news of Mr Sinclaire's passing. We are all in black here.
>
> Eliza, who reads the most peculiar things, tells me that in a house when a Jew dies (I told you this was peculiar!) everyone tears their clothes and sits on little stools because they are low with grief. Perhaps you and Mr Stanger have got through F for Funerals in the Encyclopædia so you knew that already. Every time Susannah gets up she sits down again feeling faint, so "low with grief" sounds right to me.
>
> I don't know if Eliza feels that way herself. Of course she is sorry, but I don't know if any of the girls knew Mr Sinclaire particularly well since he's been ill for so long. They are truly the <u>dearest</u> children. I would say so even were I not their aunt and partial. The older two have quite strong characters, thank goodness. (I mean I like people with strong characters. Tansy is a menace and has a wonderfully dark look. She reminds me of <u>you</u>.) Sally will have one in time—a character that is—but for now she's rather keen on dollies and not much else.
>
> It's been hard to inquire about a suitable place for Miss Green and Miss Horne under the circumstances.

Ned added, "She has crossed out something I believe is *Also I will miss Miss Green.* Instead she goes on."

> I hope you have had some luck. I know you don't like writing letters but you <u>do</u> know some people here and there. Papa is

looking for me too. But that's not to say that you shouldn't <u>as well</u>.

"Managing woman!" Ned broke in to growl.

>I don't know if you heard that I briefly had an understanding with Percy Wolcott. That is no longer the case. He wrote to Papa asking permission and dear Papa said he wished to meet him before giving it. That seemed quite fair. The meeting was delayed by circumstance however and I reconsidered. He is a very good, kind young man but we wouldn't suit. I am not sure he knows about turnips.

Ned didn't lower the letter but addressed John through it, irritable and shy at the same time.

"Do you see what I mean? John, my sister has sent you a *billet-doux* inside a letter to me in which she also discusses mourning customs and menacing children. Please tell her to keep her letters better separated."

John had a roar in his ears. He managed to say: "Even among *my* class a girl can't write to a man to whom she's not engaged."

Ned grumbled something that John thought was a deprecation on society's mores.

"In any case, she signs off there. *I will see you at Gatewood as soon as I can manage. Your loving sister, Katherine Fairwell.*"

John wondered if she usually signed *Katherine* or *Kitty*, but he couldn't ask.

Oh, he believed in Kitty. He believed in her today and tomorrow. His magnificent passionate Kitty!

But he'd made mistakes in his life. Unlike Miss Green, he *did* have regrets.

He didn't want to be someone else's regret.

It wasn't Ned he needed to have this conversation with. He wondered what had been in Miss Green's letter—and if it might tell him more. But it was too late in the evening to go find her, now.

"I'm sure we're all looking forward to seeing Miss Fairwell again," he said softly.

"Oh for crying out loud," said Ned. He glared at him, turning his head so he could get him with his good eye. He heaved a sigh. "Very well. My head hurts. Are you up to reading? Shall we revisit F for Funerary Customs in honour of late too-much-lamented Matthew Sinclaire?"

The next day John creaked his way into the saloon, where Miss Horne was embroidering a triviality and Miss Green was silently reading a copy of *Ackermann's*. The house didn't subscribe to *Ackermann's*, so John could only think it was the same copy that had been floating around the saloon for untold weeks.

John leaned on the doorframe, wishing that would help ease his back, but it didn't. Both of the ladies looked at him.

He'd hoped Miss Horne wouldn't be here. She had a bad habit of making a moue when confused, upset, or considering. She favoured him with a moue now.

"Miss Green," John wheezed, "I have a few questions for you about Miss Fairwell's plans for the gallery wing. May I have your attention for a minute?"

As usual, he couldn't tell what Miss Green was thinking. She rose at once. "Of course. Pardon me, Miss Horne."

Miss Green walked with him patiently back to the front of the house, one step at a time. They turned into the dining room.

John just managed to close the door before sitting down. "Ow." He smiled at her, embarrassed. "Sorry that took so long."

She pulled one of the other chairs around to face him and sat solemnly with her hands in her lap.

"If you had waited a few more days to become mobile, Mr Stanger, it would have been convenient. I was once again finding myself forced to plot how to escape from Miss Horne's oversight. I do not care to revisit those days. So thank you for seeing to it."

John couldn't laugh with his back hurting, but he grimaced in amusement. "Does your desire to talk to me by any chance have to do with Miss Fa—oh, hell—Kitty's letter?"

"It does." She looked down at her hands. "I should first say that when Kitty was here, she never talked to me about you."

That stabbed as much as his back. "Never?"

"Except when we first came. And only after that when required by conversation."

"But you're her friend. I thought…?"

She looked up at him. "In the same way that I never once mentioned Harry Bastable to anyone of my acquaintance."

"Oh." He was set back, having to think about that.

"She was engaged to Percy Wolcott. I believe she was being scrupulous, in the best way she knew."

"Yes—I see."

"But now, you see, I have had a letter from her." She tilted her head, amused. It was not an expression John had often seen on her face. "She told me to burn it after I was done reading it."

John blinked. That didn't seem particularly Kittyish. "That seems…quite dramatic of her."

"She was rectifying her earlier omission."

"Oh." He wished he wasn't blushing, but he couldn't help it.

Miss Green's lips quirked upwards into a smile. "It was several pages long."

Oh Kitty, Kitty, he thought desperately, some day will you tell me what was in that letter?

"Was there, ah," he struggled, "anything in particular she wanted me to know?"

"She has broken off with Percy Wolcott."

"Ned told me. Was there anything more?"

"She left it to my discretion."

She fell silent.

After a moment, John said in a strangled voice, "Is this where we find out how much you like me?"

Miss Green put back her head and laughed.

It was *certainly* the first time he'd heard her laugh. Though brief, it was a round and delighted expression of merriment, fully contradictory to her usual shy, downcast manner. For the first time he had a sense of what she might have been like in private with Bastable— uninhibited and happy to be alive. The moments that had led her to say: I regret nothing.

"I think you are a good man, Mr Stanger." She sobered, becoming quiet and still again. "Though I don't think most people would consider me a good judge of character."

"Let's suppose I am a good man," John said. "Even if not a gentleman."

"I think you're too good. If you'd ruined her and then offered to marry her I think you could have saved everyone a great deal of worry."

John raised his eyebrows. "That—may be a little excessively frank, Miss Green."

"The ability to be frank is, I am finding, the sole benefit of being a fallen woman," she said without emotion.

"Even if you have a low opinion of what men do to women, her brother is my best friend. And it seems beside the point in this case —because I don't think Kitty fancies rogues."

She nodded solemnly. "A blessing. She and I will never compete."

John wheezed a chuckle despite himself.

She said, "Would Mr Fairwell object to you marrying? Ned Fairwell, I mean."

"*Ned* doesn't matter. There's her father and three other brothers to contend with. And worst of all—a sister with daughters."

She nodded again, but also shrugged her narrow shoulders at the same time. "They all love Kitty and they will deny her nothing. If they were first and foremost worried about her reputation they would give her a companion like—" She caught herself. "Well, not like Miss Horne. *I* fooled Miss Horne, and I'm not as clever as Kitty.

The *idea* of Miss Horne."

"What do you really have to say, Miss Green? You claim to be frank, but you aren't."

"I need to repay a favour to a friend," she said softly, "by doing what I can to secure her happiness. Why do you think I have already decided how best to do that? It isn't an easy matter, and I have little reason to trust my own judgment."

John moved his unpainful arm in a gesture of acknowledgement. "You don't have to decide. But you can answer a question honestly. I am, and I think Kitty might be, stuck in *hoping*. You're outside of it. So just tell me something."

She nodded slowly. "Perhaps. What is your question?"

"The only question that matters to me. Would she be happy as my wife? Not for a week or a month. But when next year's London season starts and she gets letters from her friends about ball gowns and musical entertainments. Tales of fox hunts and horse races and Bath assemblies and parties in grand country houses owned by viscounts—to which she wasn't invited. Will she read the letters to me laughing, or keep them to herself, longingly?"

"That is a very good question," she said slowly, looking at her hands in her lap. "*Would she be happy*. That you think to ask it now speaks well of you. I don't think my parents asked it of each other. Bastable never asked it about me. And I wouldn't let myself think about it until it was almost too late.

"I don't think it's possible to know the answer, do you? But you mentioned hope.

"Some hopes are unwarranted. My most foolish hope was unwarranted. Your and Kitty's hope, though, I think—is a fair one. This might be *Better done, and regretted* than *Undone and forever unknown*.

"Even though, if that's the best we can do in life, it seems a tragedy."

John sighed.

"Do Kitty a favour," he said. "Don't write to her. Not about this. Because if she *is* going to think of anything that will make her reconsider me, I want her to do that now. I suppose that makes me a coward. But the other thing is—if you advise her, and she ends up unhappy, she'll blame you. And it'd be bad enough to unhappy in love without being unhappy in friendship at the same time."

Miss Green laughed again, softly. "I promise, Mr Stanger. But don't make me regret it."

CHAPTER EIGHTEEN

KITTY STAYED AT FORESTER House for what felt like a lifetime. She was glad she was there—but at the same time she was caught in the agonizing heartache of not being able to return to Gatewood. She wrote letters, to Ned and to Louisa.

There was nothing else she could do about that. She had other more urgent occupations. Susannah needed her.

Susannah could do nothing but sit, sometimes in silence or sometimes weeping; Kitty sent away callers and saw that Susannah ate, and she coördinated with the butler and housekeeper and made sure that all of the girls had mourning clothes that fit.

Anyone could have done those things. But no one else could have sat with Susannah alone in the evenings when she rocked back and forth and raged in a barely audible whisper about lost years and unfairness and slow dull grinding hatred. Kitty stroked her hair and let her rant.

After ten days Susannah looked at her with a start. "Are you still here?"

"Of course, Sooze."

Susannah fixed her with huge, beautiful eyes all reddened with weeping. "Wasn't there something you were supposed to do?"

She had the hesitant sound of someone waking from sleep.

Kitty didn't want her to worry. "Yes, break off my engagement with Mr Wolcott. I did that some while ago."

Susannah's mouth worked as if she had a thought on the tip of her tongue. It drifted up finally.

"Weren't you in love with someone?"

"Yes, Sooze," said Kitty gently.

"I want to tell you to throw off all men," said Susannah, "but I'd do it knowing I have the full intention of making myself a hypocrite as soon as I can. Because men are the most *beautiful* things." She breathed out. "More's the pity. So as long as you think you can do better than Matthew Sinclaire, go right now. Don't waste another moment of your youth."

"Sooze, you need me."

"I need you to *go*—and send me back a happy letter."

Kitty went home, dreamlike. No, but why was Gatewood House "home" now?

At Gatewood the drive was visible from the library windows, so Kitty was unsurprised when Ned came out into the hall just as she was taking off her gloves.

"Good day, Ned, it's so lovely to see you."

"You didn't even stay in London a whole two weeks."

"Are you disappointed?"

He didn't make any expression, only observed: "I thought your intention was to comfort Susannah."

"So it was, and I'm glad I went for so long as I did. But she sent me away."

"Oh? Did you try to rearrange *her* household too?"

"No. She thought it more important that I work on arranging my own."

Ned didn't understand for a second; then he raised his eyebrows; then he affected not to catch her meaning.

He said gruffly, "The post has just come and I'm answering letters. Shall I expect to see you at dinner?"

"Yes, please." Kitty could not wait a second more. "In the meantime, I would like to speak to Mr Stanger. Is he about?"

Howard put in: "I believe he's walked down the woods path, Miss. He should be back within the hour. Would you like me to send someone to fetch him?"

"Ah, no," said Kitty.

She found herself taking off her bonnet. It was sunny out, and she knew that to ensure her pale, fashionable complexion she ought to keep the bonnet on. But she couldn't bear to. She needed to not have so much fashion between her and the world, at that moment.

"I'll find him myself."

"Yes, Miss Fairwell," said Howard.

Ned snorted, and looked pleased, and went back into the library.

Kitty walked down the gravelled woods path with her face turned up to the late spring sun. It was hours past its zenith but still warm and bright in a clear sky. The birds were making a racket in the wood and she could smell the wonderful scents of grass and earth.

She felt now that she was in no hurry; she had all the time in the world. A feeling she never had in London, between morning calls and evening events.

The path curved around a hillock and at the bottom was where she found John Stanger on his back in the grass.

He heard her feet on the gravel and sat up. She drew near and cast her shadow across him.

"My dear Mr Stanger. Did you fall?"

He looked up at her and smiled. Oh, she'd forgotten how handsome he was. Men *were* the most beautiful things, just as Susannah had said.

"My dear Miss Fairwell. No, the grass was warm and I wanted to enjoy it."

Kitty sat facing him and stretched out her legs alongside his. "Warm and prickly. It's going to be a splendid summer."

"I'd take *anything* better than last year."

She grinned. "Spoken like a true farmer."

He leaned forward to examine her face closely. With concern, she thought.

"I've got to get something out of the way, Kitty."

"What?"

"You look terrible in black. Like Lady Death. And not in a

Goddess-like way an Ancient would have built a temple to. More as if you ought to be tucked up in bed with some warm soup."

Kitty threw back her head and howled with laughter. "Luckily, Susannah looks stunning in black. She's in mourning for a *year*. For me, she said a month was enough. I brought Ned a black armband and he says he's not wearing it."

"Is that about three weeks to go, then?"

"Yes."

He gave her a chest-to-ankle up-and-down with an expression that conveyed: "Three bad weeks, but I suppose I can use my imagination."

"You're not really ill, are you?" he asked. "It's just the dreadful clothes? You've got smudges under your eyes."

"I'm—" She frowned. "Oh, it's terribly embarrassing! I'm afraid I've been lovesick. Let's not talk of it quite yet. *You*, on the other hand, look—*very* good."

"Looks can be deceiving."

"Oh dear. What's the worst of it? Does your back hurt?"

"Often. But it's healing. Underneath. On top it's got the wildest red scar. Like a smashed apple. That would be where *you* stuck your fingers in."

She shuddered. "You know that moment sometimes still gives me the shivers at night when I think of it."

The corners of his mouth lifted and he looked at her from under his eyelashes, as if he were almost saying: Do you think *that's* why you have shivers at night?

Kitty scooted forward. "May I see?"

"It's nasty. And what a foolish reason to have a scar. This one, on the other hand—" He wasn't wearing a cravat. He wiggled down the loose collar of his shirt and leaned forward so she could see his collarbone. "Honourably gained war wound."

Kitty scooted forward some more and put her nose nearly against it. "Let me see; I can hardly see it. Looks like a scratch. You sure you weren't just picking berries?"

"Too early for good berries. And you know it, Fairwell."

She stayed where she was, nose and lips almost touching him. Her curls tickled the edge of his chin. The warmth of her breath went down his shirt.

"I've been fretting myself silly over something," she murmured.

"Don't do *that*. What is it?"

"That you won't ask me to marry you."

"Well, that is silly," he said softly.

"I've been afraid I'm going to have to ask *you*. It seems so improper."

He put his hand gently under her chin and tipped her back so he could see her eyes. "The thing is, Kitty—if I ask you if you thought it through properly, I just have to trust your answer."

She frowned at him. "Do you have some reason to think you *can't* trust my answer?"

"No. But I need to hear you say it. It shouldn't go unsaid. Am I really the kind of man you want, Kitty? Not just today, but forever. With mud on my boots and freckles from working in the sun."

She put her hand on his cheek and looked at him squarely.

"I want the kind of man whose body and mind both speak to mine," she said. "The kind of man who does not mind if I wear pretty dresses, but will still speak to me of serious things. Like friendship, and love, and barley. Especially if I find myself with fewer friends on account of deciding what I think is important. And I hope that he is a brave man, like someone who pulled his friend to safety."

He smiled ruefully. "This is a kind of bravery I'm having to work up to, Kitty. Your life has been so big and grand—"

She grinned. "And your pleasure is lying in warm and prickly grass?"

"If you want to put it that way."

"You should trust me to know where my pleasures are, Mr Stanger." She chuckled and fell backwards into the grass. He heard her voice clear. "I insist that you make me happy, John."

"Oh, *do* you!" He laughed. "I feel as if there are two ways I could take that."

"One of the reasons you make me happy is that you are so quick to catch my meaning. Come down here and one of us will be brave."

He moved around to lie in the warm and prickly grass beside her. He stroked his fingers across her curls. "Mm, let me do it," he breathed.

"I'm waiting, John Stanger."

"Katherine Fairwell, will you do me the honour of being my wife?"

She smiled up at him. "Are you only asking because I have you in a compromising position and you'd like to take advantage of it?"

"I'm asking because I would like to compromise you repeatedly for many, many years. How d'you like that?"

"I think it's a grand idea," she said. "You should start now."

They returned to the house bashfully. John kept making Kitty stop so he could pick grass out of her hair. Most of her hairpins had been declared lost causes.

In the saloon, Miss Horne glanced at them and her eyes widened. She made an exceptionally disapproving moue.

Miss Green raised her head from the *Ackermann's* she had been staring at for weeks. A smile took over her face.

"May I recommend," she said in her low clear voice, "always keeping a few spare hairpins tucked into the hem of your skirt?"

"I don't think it'll be necessary," said Kitty merrily.

Much to their shared regret, they had to part ways to dress for dinner. Kitty added a blue calico shawl over her black bombazine dinner dress in the interest of looking less like Lady Death and more like she felt—Lady Joy. She kept beaming at herself from the mirror.

Jane sighed over her hair but made it presentable.

"How do I look, Jane?"

"Like you've got the best secret in the world, Miss."

Kitty beamed again. "I don't need to have any secret at all."

"Ned, I've decided to marry Mr Stanger."

Ned looked relieved.

"Oh good. Thank you, Kitty. I promised him the upstairs as as wedding gift. Frankly, you can have the whole house except for the library."

"Oh!" said Kitty, delighted. "How wonderful that you have settled that already! I was afraid we were going to have to build another house and draw lots for it. Which is a pity, for I like this one. Especially that big rose window upstairs. And just *think* of the difficulty of finding another really good butler!

"Don't worry, Mr Stanger, I would pay for a butler out of my pin money; but I *won't* do without. I'm so sorry, you're going to have to get used to a rich wife who likes a little of everything. Please promise me your pride won't be damaged."

John had been laughing. "As long as she's you, Kitty. Besides, I've already been living in someone else's house. Do as you like when it comes to butlers."

"But Ned, if you *are* willing to share the house—" she grinned "—you can possibly have more of it than the library. For example, I *have* seen you use the dining room."

John said mildly: "We can settle the details later."

"Although," Kitty went on, still to Ned, "you *should* know I will be taking him on a tour of—hmm—how does Ireland sound to you, John? directly after the wedding."

"Ireland by all means," said John, "but it seems to me we'll have to go to Grandbourne *first*. Since your father hasn't met me, and if that's a requirement for his permission—"

"The post is slow over the distance," Ned said. "So I wrote him last week, on a chance. He's never seen Gatewood and I convinced him he'd like to see your improvements. He's looking forward to meeting you. If you have the vicar publish the banns this Sunday you can be married shortly after he gets here. Or if you want to purchase a license, I'll—"

"Banns are more than good enough for me," said Kitty firmly.

John raised his un-brows at Ned. "*Now* who's the managing one?"

"I am," said Ned. "I trusted Kitty to not be a fool. *You're* too careful."

"Well, I accepted as soon as she asked me," said John. He glanced at Kitty, who was laughing. "Or is that not how it happened?"

On their twenty-fifth wedding anniversary, John and Kitty Stanger went to London to watch the young Queen's coronation.

On their way home, they walked up a hill and admired the turnips.

* * *

THANK YOU!

Thank you for reading *A Good Kiss is Hard to Find!* Kitty and John's story is the first book of my Fearless Fairwells series. It's followed by:

Book 2: *My Heart Did Fly*, Will and Frances's story
Book 3: *Foolish Hope*, Ned and Louisa's story

Book 1.5, *The Forgotten Fiancé* is a short story about Percy Wolcott finding love after he and Kitty part ways. While I was writing *A Good Kiss*, I didn't have any particular plans to write more about Percy, but when he finally made an appearance, he was so sweet I knew at once I needed to discover his Happily Ever After. My DH (Dear Housemate) suggested a title—and the rest is history! *The Forgotten Fiancé* is available for free on my website.

If you'd like to be notified when I release new books, please sign up for my newsletter at augustinelang.com! Or you can find me as *xoxoAugustine* on Twitter, Facebook, Instagram, and BookBub.

If you think other people might enjoy Kitty and John's story, I'd be so grateful if you left a review on whatever book website you prefer. Reviews are how readers choose books, so without reviews, it can be hard for authors to find an audience.

Please turn the page to get a peek at Will and Frances's story!

EXCERPT OF *MY HEART DID FLY*

CHAPTER ONE

WILL FAIRWELL HAD LITTLE TO recommend him except money. He was neither handsome nor strapping, and he talked far, *far* too much.

His family's nickname—the Fearless Fairwells—had been earned by three heroic brothers. Will, on the other hand, had to talk himself into wearing a striped waistcoat rather than a plain one. Oh, how he hated that nickname.

He *did* have good hair. Lustrous, thick sandy-brown hair with a natural curl that so many a dandy had to work for.

At the moment, however, the hair wasn't doing him any good.

Nor, unfortunately, was the money.

The tall, broad, angry Scotsman loomed over him. "*Listen*, little man. Have ye ever been beaten to within an inch o' your life?"

"Of course!" said Will with undue cheer, happy to have a question that was easy to answer. "I went to *Eton*. Briefly."

*

Three weeks previous

He couldn't say it was entirely due to Mary Fettinger—but she had something to do with it.

Miss Fettinger, the ward of Will's cousin Mrs Whalen, was smiling too brightly at him from beneath the brim of her limp brown bonnet in the sitting-room of the Whalens' London terrace house.

Dressed for church, the young lady sat on the sofa with her

gloved hands folded demurely in her lap. The pale yellow of her muslin gown made her peaches-and-cream complexion glow. The limp brown bonnet adequately disguised her limp blonde hair. She might have presented a charming sight, had she not had fixed upon her face the glassy smile of a woman *determined* to please.

Will sat stiffly on the chair facing her, balancing as usual with the toes of his boots just touching the Turkish carpet. Outside the window behind him, he could hear the rattle of carriages as the *ton* made its way to Sunday morning services. All the brawny male Whalens of the household had already departed to those ends. Only Mrs Whalen, and Will's younger sister Kitty, had so far failed to make an appearance downstairs.

The airy sitting-room in which he and Miss Fettinger waited was full of early-morning sunshine, and furnishings in the height of taste, yet notably empty of anyone who might have served as a suitable chaperon for Miss Fettinger.

This worried Will extensively. It hadn't escaped his notice that Mrs Whalen's orphaned, penniless, prospectless ward had decided *he* was a very good prospect indeed. Although he wasn't a proud man, he was a romantic, and the idea of being married for his bank-roll made him want to cringe and run far, far away.

Not that Miss Fettinger was not a pleasant young lady. She was. Indeed, she always listened to his babblings with the *most* pleasant of expressions. That was how he knew. The people who cared about him told him to shut up sometimes.

Yet he was both too polite to desert a lady, and too much of a coward to flee from one when he should.

"That is an interesting hat," was how he began nervously, after they had expended all possible discussion of how surprisingly pleasant the weather was for April.

Mary Fettinger smiled even more brightly. Too late, Will remembered that any comment on a lady's attire would have to be taken as a certain type of attention.

"Do you like it, Mr Fairwell?" she inquired in her sweet, earnest voice.

He back-peddled. "It is very…fine. And large. I'm not sure I have opinions about ladies' hats, if you'll forgive me."

She nodded graciously.

But could he stop there? No. His tongue kept going. His brother Robert said that he talked at a trot.

"But it does worry me, a little. It looks as if it would not keep the rain off your hair, or not for long, which seems a problem for a hat, as I believe that's what they're for."

"It is a hat for clear days," explained Mary Fettinger, her earnesty as unflinching as her smile.

"Oh! So it is a special-occasion hat. A risky special-occasion hat. You are daring, Miss Fettinger. I think of a hat as being a protective mechanism, something one does not technically always *need*, except for the sake of tradition, but when you do need it, you need it at once, so it is best to have one with you at all times. Which is why I still don't see the point of non-waterproof hats, I suppose. Can you explain?"

"It is because it is pretty."

"*Is* it?" Will drew himself up short. He wouldn't go so far as to insult her, even through accidentally slighting her foolish hat. "Oh! Yes. Of course it is. It's too bad men don't get to wear hats because they are pretty, or perhaps it's just as well—that would be another way for me to be hopelessly lost in fashion. I suppose I could wear a cocked hat rather than a tall one but I can't say either is *prettier* than the other."

"I suppose not," she murmured valiantly.

"Not that it matters; a pretty hat on my head would be gilding a sow's ear," he added in retrospect.

Will was exaggerating. He was better-looking than a sow's ear. But it *was* true that he was no lady's ideal specimen. Most ladies preferred their gentlemen to be taller than themselves, for example. Or, even if not tall, at least built in a way that signified masculine strength—rather than looking as if they could be carried away by a strong breeze. Fencing and gymnastics had hardly helped.

Kitty was kind: she had declared he had a heart-shaped face. What she meant was that he had a breadth of forehead and a face that narrowed to a distinctly pointy chin. His nose also was sharply pointed, like a fox's. His friend Allen said the whole gave him a "devilish aspect," but when Will looked in the mirror it seemed to him that his eyebrows and mouth looked perpetually worried, and he doubted devils worried about much.

H e *did* grant that the worried expression might be due to his feelings about mirrors. When he smiled, a crooked upper tooth hung over his lower lip.

He liked smiling, so he avoided mirrors.

Miss Fettinger seemed to be aware that a compliment or at least a disagreement was needed, but she seemed at a loss for words. There was a few second's gap in the conversation.

Which he immediately filled.

"Have you ever read what Hippocrates had to say about the weather? Well, I imagine not, as ladies are assumed to be interested in hats rather than Hippocrates—but perhaps it has come under your eye somehow?"

He could see in Mary Fettinger's face a flicker of horrified realization. Then she composed herself at once.

"I have never had the pleasure of reading Hippocrates, Mr Fairwell."

"Well, I'm not sure I'd call it a *pleasure*. For pleasure we might all be better off studying hats. But there's probably something to be learned from him. He observed, you see, that if you know about the winds and exposure of a city, you can know which diseases to which the citizens will be most subject."

"Did you study medicine, Mr Fairwell? I did not know."

"Oh, no. No stomach for it. In fact I almost became a clergyman but, ah, I didn't. But my brother Robert told me when I was a boy that if I couldn't manage to keep quiet, I should at least read to find varied topics of conversation."

She made what seemed to him to be an inadvertent expression of astonishment. Perhaps she had thought him unaware of his own tendencies.

Then she smoothed her face once again.

"I am sure that made you quite popular at Oxford," she said with polite blankness.

Will laughed, then wasn't sure if she were joking, so he stopped.

"Well, I suppose the reactions of strangers to my character are a useful sign as to whether I should be friends with them."

Miss Fettinger continued to look blank. Will turned himself back to Hippocrates, feeling that his school days were left well enough alone.

"I do wish he'd given examples. Hippocrates. Not Robert. Of the cities, I mean. He got quite exhaustive about the diseases. It's easy enough to see whether a city lies to the north or the south or the east or west—though perhaps not; London lies to the south-east of England, but compared to the Continent it is relatively rather north-west. I think we should leave out America, don't you? It complicates things even more."

He paused for a second, because he could see the exact instant when her eyes glazed over.

Yet instead of saying, "Oh, who *cares*," which was what she so clearly felt, she said, with the frozen smile: "I'm sure you know best, Mr Fairwell."

"I wouldn't bet on it," he murmured.

Usually, once he saw the eyes glaze, he would switch topics. He had plenty to choose from. He was a hopeless chatterbox, but he did try so very hard not to be a bore.

And yet, and yet…he *was* trying to put her off, wasn't he? He took a deep breath and let loose.

"I don't fully understand much of what he says, for one thing. Possibly that is my failure at the Greek, or at the translation I cribbed from when I gave up on the Greek. Sometimes he is talking about cities, and sometimes about tribes, and sometimes about countries, so it's hard to sort him out. It *does* come clear when he is talking about Greece. The worse he has to say is that his countrymen are hairy and opinionated. But naturally they are 'acute and ingenious in the arts and military matters.'"

"Naturally," said Miss Fettinger.

There was something about her shift of weight that made Will think she wanted to speak.

And, blast it, he was polite enough to shut up.

Miss Fettinger gathered herself. "It is so pleasant of you to walk with us to church, Mr Fairwell. I must own I cannot regret whatever it is that delays my guardian and your sister. You and I have scarcely had a moment to converse in weeks. Indeed, I was concerned I had given you offence in some way. Your sister disclaimed it, but perhaps you would not confide. You *would* tell me if I had done, wouldn't you?"

Will looked at her in terror.

He didn't blame Miss Fettinger for setting her eye on him. After all, he did have money, and he lacked vices, other than the babbling. He wouldn't beat her, or even importune her if she claimed a headache.

He couldn't *blame* her—but quite against his will, he held a resentment against her. If she needed money, he would rather just give it to her and *not* marry her. He could too easily envision how she would treat him with infinite forbearance, in a you-are-my-cross-to-bear sort of way. He would rather be alone.

Most of the time. Much of the time.

There were moments when he weakened. There had been that one Sunday some weeks ago, when they'd all been walking together, and Mrs Whalen's eldest daughter's utterly adorable brats had clambered all over him.

He had come so close to proposing to Miss Fettinger at that moment, because then they could have their *own* adorable brats, who, one hoped, would have his hair and her everything else. But then he had imagined the chaste, tidy little kisses Miss Fettinger, as Mrs Fairwell, would have given him—as his due. And he could think of nothing more dreadful.

That was when he'd extracted Kitty's promise not to leave him alone with her.

He had *not* told Kitty how he was pretty certain the only reason Mrs Whalen, who was quite a distant cousin indeed, had agreed to host Kitty for her coming-out was that Mrs Whalen could use it as a way of tossing Miss Fettinger in his path.

"Of course not," he said.

Miss Fettinger looked confused. "Of course you would not tell me, or of course I have done you no offence?"

He was too much of a coward to either lie or tell the truth.

"As you've pointed out, Miss Fettinger, we've hardly spoken. Where could you even have had the opportunity?"

She kept looking confused.

Fortunately, at that moment, there was a clatter in the hall. His little sister Kitty entered, tying her bonnet over her curly chestnut hair which was already creeping out of its hairpins. They shared their hair and small statures, but luckily for her, not much resemblance of face. She was a beautiful young lady with a vivacious expression.

"Oh, Will! I'm so sorry to keep you waiting. Mrs Whalen took a dislike to my frock, saying it either not simple enough for church, or not fine enough, I'm sure I don't know. And then after changing I needed a new shawl, and she desired to find me one of hers. She is so kind."

Kitty smiled at him. Will swallowed a laugh. Perhaps Kitty had caught on to what Mrs Whalen was up to, after all.

"And now she's—oh, I hardly know! What were you and Miss Fettinger speaking of? May I join you?"

Kitty had an angelic face and a wicked sense of humour.

"Hippocrates," said Will with a sigh.

Kitty looped her arm around Will's, neatly circumventing any future attempt of Miss Fettinger to do the same.

"Oh, *please!* Not Hippocrates! I could hardly bear it. You will have to tell me later, when we won't bore dear Miss Fettinger. Bless your forbearance, Miss Fettinger!"

Kitty would protect him from gold-diggers as much as she could—but that didn't mean she wouldn't have her fun as well.

"I'm sure I don't understand," said Mary Fettinger. She appeared to steel herself. "Please go on, Mr Fairwell. Did Hippocrates have any insights about our own fair country?"

"*That* was when I said I had to give up looking for Britain in his description because I realized that at the time he was writing, we were a bunch of barbaric heathens."

"Oh, well done, Will!" said Mrs Campinari.

His friend and fellow whist-aficionado smiled at him over her cards. The many and gaudy rings on her long fingers flashed in the light of the candles affixed to the four corners of the small gaming-table. It was quite late at night, and whilst the four whist-players sat in a circle of light, around them the cramped space of the small sitting-room was hidden in shadow.

"*Was* it well-done, though? I don't know. I feel cruel putting her off."

"That's just what she's depending on," drawled their third player, Miss Regina Hampton.

Regina was a lovely, slightly-past-her-youth lady with arched dark eyebrows and a mass of jet-black hair, which she most improperly insisted on wearing down in her own home. It slid over the shoulders of her dark green silk banyan, throwing small gleams in the candlelight.

Will had met Regina through his friend Tom Rutherford. Initially he'd had doubts about their relationship—but the obvious love she and Tom shared for each other had put his doubts to rest.

"If you marry her, I'll disown you," said Rutherford now.

Rutherford was one of the few fellow students Will had met at Oxford whose eyes did *not* glaze over. Or, when they started to, he could defend himself with an amiable "Hush."

He was tall and strapping in the way that Will was not. Will tried not to be envious. He comforted himself with the way Rutherford's moustache, about which he was exceptionally vain, was prematurely greying.

The thrice-widowed but still spritely Mrs Campinari had once been Rutherford's sister-in-law, though Rutherford had been a schoolboy at the time. They argued now and then if she were *still* his sister-in-law even after the brother had died. Or if she had remained so after remarrying. Regardless, her friendship with Rutherford had outlasted the husbands.

Despite the array of jewelled rings not altogether in the best of taste, Mrs Campinari's grey-sprinkled light brown hair was tucked under a proper lacy cap, and her peach cotton-and-silk gown draped elegantly over her tall, slim form. Not only her fingers, but everything about Mrs Campinari was long and slim—long limbs, a long nose, a long neck slightly sagging. With her habit of wearing peach, beige, and pink, she at times put Will in mind of a flamingo.

"I don't think you can disown friends, even if they marry people you don't like," Will observed, "since you don't own them to start with. You can only cut them."

"Besides," said Mrs Campinari, "then we would have to find another friend of good character and tolerant morals to be our fourth. It is *not* to be thought of."

"We wouldn't have to cut him," Regina said archly. "She would find out—because Will would tell her—that he's playing whist with an *actress* in a trysting-place. And that would be the end of that."

"Doesn't it matter that you aren't *my* mistress?"

"No," said Mrs Campinari, Rutherford, and Regina simultaneously.

"I suppose not," Will sighed. "Well, I will just have to find a girl who doesn't mind my incessant babbling and funny face—ow!" That because Mrs Campinari had smacked him on the arm, but he continued "—*and* has tolerant morals. Is tolerant really the word we should be using here?"

"Just as long as she doesn't want to *play* whist with us," said Rutherford. "You'd have to sit out; sorry, Will. See if you can find a perfect girl who likes *watching* card-playing."

"At the moment, I would be satisfied with not accidentally proposing to Mary Fettinger."

"I certainly don't think you should be left alone with her," said Mrs Campinari. "She might get desperate."

Will groaned. "Oh, blast. Next week I'm going to arrange to be out of town on Sunday. I know I promised Kitty, but she seems to be doing all right without me. I'll take her driving instead."

"But not tomorrow," said Rutherford. "Tomorrow, we have a box at the Drury Lane. It's *Othello*, which I know stirs your romantic instincts, and the after-piece is reputed to be a howler. It'll keep you from getting glum, despite the Mary Fettingers of the world."

Will was happy about the change of topic, and they all switched to talking about the theatre. But Regina was still giving him a thoughtful look over the top of her cards.

CHAPTER TWO

THE WHIST GAME WAS ENDED inconclusively at eleven o'clock by the arrival of Mrs Campinari's carriage. It was hardly a quarter-hour's walk from Regina's flat to Mrs Campinari's Mayfair home, but she preferred not to risk her dignity, her reticule, or her rings, even with Will to escort her. Will couldn't argue that he was not the most imposing escort.

Mrs Campinari had long established that she would arrange things to her own satisfaction, and they didn't live so far apart, so Will prepared to depart with her in her carriage.

As Mrs Campinari was hunting for a missing glove, and Rutherford was assisting, Regina came up to Will.

"Will," she said softly, and pressed his hand. "Promise me you won't marry a girl who doesn't love you."

He was startled. He couldn't say that he absolutely had not been thinking about it.

"There's a young lady out there for you—I promise." She smiled crookedly. "I know that is a terribly romantic thing for a woman like me to say. But perhaps, having had a few patrons, and only now realized what it was like to be in love, I can speak for the importance of it. So swear to me."

"That is an awfully large thing to promise," said Will. "I agree in theory, but I'm going to be twenty-six soon and at a certain point I think I might have to stop being romantic. Can I promise for the next two years? And then marry whomever the Mary Fettinger is in 1815?"

Regina frowned and shook her head with a sharp swish of hair. "Don't be as practical as a woman has to be. You are not a hopeless case; you simply haven't been lucky yet. Swear to me—or I'll call Tom and Mrs C over to witness it as well, and you'll be even more embarrassed."

"That is positively unkind of you."

She arched her dark eyebrows at him, waiting.

Will thought about the difference between Mary Fettinger's glazed-over eyes, and the way Regina Hampton and Tom Rutherford looked at each other. He took a deep breath.

"Very well. I swear I will not marry a woman who doesn't love me enough to tell me to shut up when I'm boring her."

She squeezed his hand and released it. "I hear your vow, Mr Fairwell."

"However—in two years I reserve the right to a fair and merciful hearing. You can't deny me that."

"I am confident it will not be necessary."

"Will, are you ready?" called Mrs Campinari.

He fetched his hat and walking-stick. "Yes, Mrs C. At your convenience."

Mrs Campinari was ignorant of his parting conversation with Regina, so during the carriage ride she mused about the Viscount Chillwick. The Viscount was her own latest romance, though he was not yet aware of it.

Will was all too happy to oblige her choice of topic.

When the carriage stopped, a bleary-eyed footman handed Mrs Campinari down. Will hopped out after her.

Mrs Campinari's astonishing, ornate Italianate mansion loomed over a block of well-behaved English terraces. She and her friends called it the Palazzino as a joke.

"Have a good night, Mrs C. I'll walk the rest of the way. It's a fine evening."

The footman looked hopeful.

"Are you certain?" worried Mrs Campinari.

"My fencing lessons are going well," Will said cheerfully. "If anyone tries to mug me—I'll throw my cane at him and run the other way."

"Perhaps Jack should go with you."

From the footman's resigned expression, he was Jack.

"No, no. I'll see you tomorrow for the theatre. Have a pleasant evening." Will tipped his hat, then grinned at Jack, including him in the motion.

It *was* a fine evening, and peaceful, though he kept a careful eye out and a tight grip on his walking-stick.

The Fairwells did own a house in London, but his sister Susannah lived there. Since her husband was perpetually on the edge of dying, it had a gloomy atmosphere. Will spent a fair amount of time in Forester House spoiling his nieces and trying to cheer up his sister, but he didn't want to live there. A spacious hotel suite seemed quite ample enough for a bachelor—and it saved the need for hiring staff.

Some of the other members of his club made fun of him for being a skinflint. He always did his best to explain that being a skinflint was the only way to hold on to a fortune once you had one. That was a point not commonly comprehended among young men, he'd found.

His three brothers had gone off to fight Boney and be heroes. Will was a coward. He'd stayed home…and organized the family's account-books.

When he'd been younger, he'd felt guilty about it. Then he'd realized that what he was doing was making sure that Kitty, and Susannah's three daughters, and *their* future daughters would always have roofs over their heads and enough to eat—even if they married useless men, or didn't marry at all.

It was a dreadfully boring and unheroic thing. It still, in his opinion, needed to be done.

His father was a competent estate manager—when he wasn't in the doldrums: but that was more often than not. Robert, technically the eldest son, was off Heaven knew where, and Ned was sulking at Gatewood House after his injuries.

That had left Will at Grandbourne to oversee the steward, check the figures, and try not to let his father's doldrums infect him too. The words "thankless work" had never been so appropriate. But it *was* better than getting shot at.

For the sake of his own sanity and to see his friends, he usually spent at least part of the Season in London. This year, since he was keeping an eye on Kitty, he had an excuse to stay the whole time.

He arrived at his hotel without incident. No one stirred when he entered his sitting-room and then passed on to his bedroom. His valet was stone-deaf—Will could have set off fireworks and Astley would never have noticed.

Henry Astley was the brother of one of Will's school friends. It had been fortuitous happenstance that the friend had mentioned his worries about how his brother would support himself, at the same time as Will had been contemplating the need for a valet.

The arrangement had worked out even better than expected. Will found it comforting to know that he never had to fear distracting or boring Astley no matter how much he nattered on at home. He did not yet have sufficient fluency in sign-language that he could be tedious in it.

(Yet. The day would probably come, and woe unto Astley.)

His friends—or rather, acquaintances—also made fun of him for being soft-hearted; as, for example, when he preferred to undress and hang up his own clothes by the light of a candle, rather than waking Astley.

Besides, he thought belatedly as he landed in bed: at some point there *would* be something he thought it worthwhile to spend a lot of money on. It just hadn't happened yet.

Perhaps in 1815 he would need to buy a house.

The next morning he swallowed his pride long enough to roust up his most stylish friend, Charles Sudbury, and enlist his help. Will felt ridiculous when even remotely dandified, but, after recently paying the breathtaking bills for Kitty's gowns, the cost of a new coat for himself seemed negligible by comparison.

And perhaps, he thought, if he could catch the eyes of *more* ladies, he would have more chances to find one who was amused by him.

It was an unsophisticated plan, but at least it was a plan.

"Since when do you want *my* advice?" inquired Sudbury as they strolled toward Bond Street.

"Well," said Will bravely, "I want a green coat."

Sudbury fell about, clutching his chest and miming a heart attack. "By stars! You? A coloured coat? Are you mad? Are you in love?"

Will didn't dignify that with an answer.

"I want a green coat," he said stubbornly, "and I've wanted one for a while; but as soon as I walk into the tailor's I'll turn into a coward and order another black one."

"You are a tough case, my friend."

"And that is why you're here!"

The coat took the whole of the morning. Will only laughed a few times when the tailor paid him compliments. Sudbury finally approved the order, shook Will's hand gravely in congratulations, and then departed to keep an appointment.

Will fetched Hippocrates and went to dine at his club, Boodle's, in hopes that he would run across someone either cleverer than he, or simply more confident with his Greek. But he kept his eye on the clock. After all, he was looking forward to *Othello*.

When Rutherford had said "we have a box" at the Theatre Royal, Drury Lane, what he meant was that Will would pay for their seats *in* a box, Mrs Campinari would provide the carriage, and Regina would not be attending.

For one, Regina was herself performing that evening, at one of the less grand theatres down the street from the Theatre Royal. The other three had seen her in that part already, so she wouldn't count them disloyal for frequenting another playhouse.

For another, it was a qualification of her relationship with Rutherford that they could not be seen in public together. His family had taut purse-strings and stringent morals. Actresses, as everyone knew, were practically prostitutes.

Never mind that Rutherford and Regina were positively domestic together.

Rutherford grumbled about it; Regina only shrugged sadly.

So it was just Rutherford, Mrs Campinari, and Will, shuffling into the red velvet seats of a box.

As always, Will had insisted they come early. He could not, as he would have wished, add eight or nine inches to his height, but he could arrive early and get a good seat. He was not as dedicated a theatre-goer as Rutherford or Mrs Campinari, but if he *were* going to attend, he wanted to *see*.

Of course, that meant he would disappoint some courtesan or dandy who wanted the front row in order to be *seen*.

The theatre glimmered gold and green in the light of many chandeliers. Wax dripped down on the mass of people seated on benches in the pit. The stage was also lit by two Argand oil lamps on handsome tripods, a new addition when the theatre had been rebuilt not long before. The brightness of the lamps had taken some getting used to, but Will liked being able to see all the minute expressions of the actors.

"Oh, Will," said Mrs Campinari, inspecting the playbill, "have you seen Miss MacDougal perform yet?"

"Of course he has!" said Rutherford.

"I beg to differ," said Will with a smile. "I would remember seeing any lady's name printed quite so bold along the top of the bill. It positively shouts its introduction. MISS MacDOUGAL as Desdemona. I believe Othello and Iago will have to team up against her. Does Miss MacDougal warrant a size of letters to rival a Mrs Siddons or a Mrs Jordan?"

"How can you *not* have seen her?" huffed Rutherford. "She's been with the Drury Lane since the beginning of the Season."

"That's all well; I seem to have missed her. It can only be your own fault, as I let you decide what we are watching, and this year it has been the Little Drury most of the time."

With strangers and passing acquaintances crowded around them in the box, he wouldn't so much as mention Regina's name, and Rutherford's reason for preferring her theatre.

"Well—that's a pity," said Rutherford after a moment.

"Let us say, rather, that it is a delight," said Mrs Campinari firmly, "because you have a treat ahead of you. I would not say that Miss MacDougal *challenges* Mrs Siddons—"

"That's good. Mrs Siddons seems like she'd eat challengers for breakfast. All the while smiling and declaiming a soliloquy."

"But she *is* a talented young lady. And very beautiful."

"Aren't they all," said Will dryly.

"I'm michtily glad to see that one of my countrywomen is making sich a success here," said Rutherford, putting on a Scottish burr.

Will and Mrs Campinari laughed at him. Rutherford had been raised in London, and sounded like it.

It was time. One of the doors on stage opened, and Roderigo and Iago entered. Will put his elbows on the railing of the box.

Rutherford and Mrs Campinari settled down. Mrs Campinari worked her fan. The other inhabitants of the box continued to talk. That was nothing out of the ordinary: but one of them had a piercing voice that cut over the opening lines with information about the voice's cousin's new horse.

"*Shhh,*" said Will. "Have some respect. It's Shakespeare."

"Sort of," muttered Rutherford. He and Mrs Campinari had been placing civilized bets in the carriage as to how much would be cut. Iago's line about "the beast with two backs" never made it in, but there was some leeway elsewhere.

Midway through Act I, Scene 3, the most beautiful woman in the world entered stage right.

Will couldn't say there had been other woman he'd seen and immediately been able to say, "Well, *there* is the woman I'm going to dream about for the next year."

There was a first time for everything.

Miss Frances MacDougal was youthful, but not a maiden in the first blush: her clear voice and confident presence could never have belonged to a girl. She was a Desdemona or a Portia, not a Juliet.

Her features, too, were strong and expressive. Her form was slim, but not lacking in well-placed curves. Dark red-brown hair entwined with a strand of pearls made her snowy skin seem even more luminous in the lamplight. The crimson, vaguely Roman dress she wore displayed a single white shoulder.

Will had not previously thought that shoulders were erotic, but hers was.

She was beautiful: but all of the actresses were beautiful.

It was the smile—a loving, knowing curve of full lips and warm eyes—which she turned toward Othello—and which Will caught almost full on in the box behind him—that turned him into a quivering jelly.

"I am hitherto your daughter," said Desdemona to Brabantio—sweetly, but with a touch of tartness to it:

"but here's my husband,
And so much duty as my mother show'd
To you, preferring you before her father,
So much I challenge that I may profess
Due to the Moor my lord."

"Oh," said Will, catching the smile. He had been dealt a killing blow.

"*Shhh,*" said the woman with the piercing voice.

After Desdemona departed the scene, Will's attention to the play parted along with her. But since he did generally watch quietly, his friends had no cause to comment when he continued to sit with his elbows on the railing looking down at the stage. They had no way of knowing that his ill-behaved mind had followed the actress into the Green Room.

What did she do there? Did she fuss with her gown? Did she converse with the other actors whilst awaiting her cue? Was she so cool-headed that she read a book? Or did she perhaps flirt with a beau?

Iago's speech caught him.

"—why, the
power and corrigible authority of this lies in our

wills. If the balance of our lives had not one
scale of reason to poise another of sensuality, the
blood and baseness of our natures would conduct us
to most preposterous conclusions: but we have
reason to cool our raging motions, our carnal
stings, our unbitted lusts, whereof I take this that
you call love to be a sect or scion."

Will took that as a scolding. He sat up straight and swallowed
his sighs.

After Iago exited, the artfully painted backdrop representing the
Duke's council chamber rolled away, revealing a seaport in Cyprus,
all stormy sky and wave. Will tried not to wait too impatiently for
Desdemona's return.

Desdemona entered, and her eyes were fierce—but she was
silent.

Unfamiliar with every line, Will didn't realize what had
happened until he discerned the murmur and motion of Mrs Campinari and Rutherford behind and beside him.

Mrs Campinari had won a bet, it seemed: and it was Desdemona
who had lost out. Her raillery with Iago and Emilia at the beginning
of Act II had been cut, and the scene patched together to cover it.

Will was dreadfully disappointed. He would have liked to see
the beautiful Scotswoman playing comedy.

He agreed with Cassio: "She is indeed perfection."

"What do you think of Miss MacDougal?" Mrs Campinari said with
delight after the play was over and they were waiting for the after-
piece. "Isn't she marvellous? It's too bad they've hacked her part to
pieces."

"She *is* marvellous," agreed Will in a nervous understatement.
Miss MacDougal had refused to die prettily at Othello's hands and
the horror of the struggle had made the entire audience weep. Will
had clung to the gallery railing reminding himself that it was neither
necessary nor possible to scramble over it and flounder through the

pit to the stage in order to rescue her.

Mostly recovered now, he told himself it was *perfectly* ordinary that he would ask his friends about the young lady's career. Mrs Campinari was always delighted to have the opportunity to draw upon her encyclopædic knowledge of the theatre. He had only to make one comment, anything leading—

He hit upon something obvious.

"If she's Scottish, she seems to have successfully rid herself of her accent. Where was she born?"

"Edinburgh," said Mrs Campinari, and then dropped her fan. "Oops!"

Rutherford searched for the fan. Will searched for the fan. Finally the lady sitting beside them deigned to twitch her skirt to the side, and the fan was recovered.

But, to his horror, Mrs Campinari began to grumble about the number of fans she lost in a year, rather than resuming the topic.

Will felt as if *everyone in the world* were looking at him when he swallowed and tried again.

"I beg your pardon, Mrs C. Where did you say Miss MacDougal was from?"

"Oh, excuse me. She was born and raised in Edinburgh." Mrs Campinari's eyebrows shot up. "Oh! Will, would you like to meet her?"

It was good that his heart was sound, or it would have stopped in its tracks.

As it was, he lost his power of speech and felt his face turn hot.

Rutherford had chanced to look at him. He began to laugh.

"Let's take that for a 'yes,' Mrs C," said Rutherford.

"I…didn't realize you were acquainted with her," Will said, making an effort to sound nonchalant even if his blush had given him away.

Mrs Campinari smiled at him sympathetically.

"Not *yet*. Mrs Hight invited me to a soirée next week and was bragging discreetly in my ear that Miss MacDougal is going to attend. From all accounts, the young lady is nice about what invitations she accepts. At least, Mrs Hight considered her acceptance quite the coup. If you would like, I'm *certain* I could secure a welcome for you as my escort."

Will managed to say, "You astonish me. I only asked where she was from and now you're inviting me to someone else's party."

"That is how things happen, my dear," said Mrs Campinari with a smile. "Oh, don't blush; we won't tease you. We *know* she is very pretty. You have every right to admire her."

"May we start," said Will hopelessly, "with some little trifle of biography? Which is really all I asked for?"

"She is twenty-three, I think, the daughter of—" she hesitated "—well, some sort of shopkeeper—but a very *respectable* man from all accounts. The profiles of her in the papers are all wonderfully flattering. And you *know* how they are if they smell any scent of impropriety. She began on the stage seven or eight years ago, I believe; she made a greater and greater success before being invited to join the Drury Lane this season. Tom and I saw her earlier as Cordelia. She was *superb*."

"Good comic timing, too," said Rutherford. "Do you remember that awful after-piece…?"

"Oh, *that*." Mrs Campinari grimaced. "What a script."

"The scene with the pie, though…. You had to pick me up off the floor." Rutherford started chuckling at the memory. "I think you were at Almack's that night, Will."

"Oh, yes. I *do* remember you telling me about the scene with the pie. Extensively. That was her?"

"It was."

"In that case, this is the first time I can say, I am very sorry I missed it."

* end of excerpt *

Made in the USA
Middletown, DE
29 April 2021